"Unless I'm out on a call, I'll be here to pick you up. And if I'm still out with my crew, I'll send one of my brothers. You're not doing any more of this on your own."

Mark's hands tightened on her hips, pulled her closer. "Do you know how much I need you to be safe? How much it kills me to know that you don't feel safe in your own home? On your own land?"

Amy reached up to stroke her fingertips across the taut angles of his cheek and jaw. She brushed her fingers across his stubbled skin, once, twice, again, until she felt the tension in his expression ease. "Nine in the morning?"

"I'll be here."

CRIME SCENE COVER-UP

USA TODAY Bestselling Author
JULIE MILLER

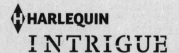

For Lissanne Jones, a fellow author, reader and friend. She sent me the generous gift of a tea sampler from Australia. I had so much fun trying the different selection of teas that I'd never seen before, much less tasted. I appreciate your kindness. Thank you!

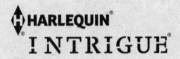

HARLEQUIN®
INTRIGUE®

PLEASE RECYCLE

THIS PRODUCT IS RECYCLABLE

Recycling programs for this product may not exist in your area.

ISBN-13: 978-1-335-13619-0

Crime Scene Cover-Up

Copyright © 2020 by Julie Miller

This edition published by arrangement with Harlequin Books S.A.

For questions and comments about the quality of this book, please contact us at CustomerService@Harlequin.com.

Harlequin Enterprises ULC
22 Adelaide St. West, 40th Floor
Toronto, Ontario M5H 4E3, Canada
www.Harlequin.com

Printed in U.S.A.

Julie Miller is an award-winning *USA TODAY* bestselling author of breathtaking romantic suspense—with a National Readers' Choice Award and a Daphne du Maurier Award, among other prizes. She has also earned an *RT Book Reviews* Career Achievement Award. For a complete list of her books, monthly newsletter and more, go to juliemiller.org.

Books by Julie Miller

Harlequin Intrigue

The Taylor Clan: Firehouse 13

Crime Scene Cover-Up

The Precinct

Beauty and the Badge
Takedown
KCPD Protector
Crossfire Christmas
Military Grade Mistletoe
Kansas City Cop

The Precinct: Bachelors in Blue

APB: Baby
Kansas City Countdown
Necessary Action
Protection Detail

Rescued by the Marine
Do-or-Die Bridesmaid
Personal Protection
Target on Her Back
K-9 Protector

Visit the Author Profile page at Harlequin.com.

CAST OF CHARACTERS

Mark Taylor—This next-generation Taylor Clan hero has followed in his adoptive parents' footsteps and become a KCFD firefighter. But after failing to save the family member he was closest to, he questions whether he can stop the arson fires threatening Kansas City and protect the quirky beauty who is caught up in the middle of the devastation.

Amy Hall—With a shed full of welding equipment and found treasures from ditches and dumpsters, this artist is seen by most people as a free spirit who marches to the beat of her own muse. But when a friend goes missing and her gran's historic home is threatened by the fires, she'll do whatever is necessary—even team up with a confoundedly sexy, bossy rule lover like Mark Taylor—to save them.

Comfort Hall—Amy's widowed grandmother, who raised her.

Jocelyn Brunt—A grad student conducting environmental research on Amy's property.

Dale O'Brien—The contractor owns the Copper Lake subdivision and has made no secret of the fact he wants the Hall women to sell him their adjoining land.

Brad & Richie—Two handymen Amy hires to help renovate her grandmother's historic farm home.

Gerald Sanders—Amy's tenant.

Derek Roland—Jocelyn's fellow researcher.

Chapter One

Mark Taylor loved the scents of fish, grill smoke and the outdoors that clung to his clothes and filled up the cab of his truck. He and the silver-haired man sitting in the passenger seat across from him were chasing the sunset along Highway 7, speeding home to Kansas City after their annual camping-and-fishing weekend at Truman Lake.

The scenery on either side of the twisting highway was especially picturesque in the summer. The rolling hills were carpeted with endless green trees giving way to tiny towns, the steel-gray water of wind-whipped lakes and the grittier browns of creeks and rivers filled with the rain that had flooded parts of the state earlier that year. Although some of the highway had been straightened and expanded into dual lanes, Mark preferred the narrower cuts of the two-lane sections because it still felt like he was out in the country. As much as he loved Kansas City, where he'd grown up and now worked as a firefighter/EMT, there was something inherently relaxing about the slower pace of the countryside.

And something good for his soul in sharing another memorable one-on-one weekend with his grandfather, Sid Taylor.

The two men had been doing this for twenty-three years, since Mark's fifth birthday. Grandpa Sid had done more than teach him how to pitch a tent or fish. As the youngest of four adopted brothers, with five uncles, an aunt and their families, it had been easy to get lost in the boisterous shuffle of holiday gatherings and Sunday dinners when the entire Taylor clan got together. But Sid had singled him out as his baby boy—his little buddy who shared his love of the outdoors. If Sid hadn't closed his butcher shop a few years back, Mark might have considered learning the trade so that he could take over his grandfather's business. Instead, he'd followed in his adoptive parents' and birth brother Matt's footsteps, and joined the KCFD.

As a little boy, Sid had made Mark feel like his favorite kid on the whole planet. Mark now knew that Sid had singled out each of his grandchildren to develop a special bond with, but he wouldn't trade these twenty-three years with his grandfather for another Chiefs Super Bowl victory. Their conversations over the years had been about nothing and everything. Sid had been there through the insecurities of getting to know his new family and measuring up to his overachieving brothers' standards; his concerns for his extremely withdrawn brother, Matt; some messy teenage angst; and the ignominy and heartache of his girlfriend saying no to his proposal and moving away to pursue a dream he wasn't invited to be a part of.

This afternoon's conversation was no different as they segued from the Royals trading away good players and relying too much on their farm system, to probing questions about whether Mark had started seeing anyone again, and on to a friendly debate about the success of their time at the lake.

"That bass was over twenty inches," Mark insisted, adjusting his wraparound sunglasses on the bridge of his nose. "Maybe even two feet."

"The one that broke your fishing line or the one in your imagination?"

Mark grinned, refusing to take that gibe without giving back one of his own. "My largemouth was twice as big as that shrimp of a striper you caught."

"Why don't you just make him a mile long now, so he doesn't have to keep getting bigger every time you tell that story," Sid teased, pulling his ball cap lower on his forehead to shield his eyes from the bright June sun.

When Mark had been a boy, his grandfather had planned the weekend to his lake of choice, packed the food and driven him—filling the time with jokes and deeper conversations about life, answering questions and challenging him to make good, thoughtful decisions about any problems he might have confided in the older man.

Now that Sid had survived two heart events, the knuckles of his workingman's hands had knotted with arthritis and his broad shoulders had stooped with age, their roles had reversed. Mark planned, packed, drove. Although he still let Sid, a retired butcher and former marine, clean the fish and grill them because there were some talents the old man had that he'd never be able to surpass. He could only emulate. Like his adoptive father had before him, like his uncles and brothers had. Every man in the Taylor family had learned about hard work, honor and integrity from this guy who was still teasing Mark about his lousy lack of fish this weekend.

"I'm just sayin' my cooler has six crappie and that eighteen-inch bass on ice to show your grandma." Sid pointed his thumb to the camper on the back of Mark's truck. "Yours is, what? Holding dirty laundry?"

"Fine. I surrender. You get the Taylor Prize for Best Fisherman this year." Mark rested his elbow on the door beside him as they crested a hill and drove down into the valley where the next creek flowed. "It's a good thing I love you, old man. I wouldn't put up with this kind of trash talk from anyone else."

"Right back at ya, son." With a drawn-out sigh, Sid sank back against his seat, looking out the side window at the pin oaks and pines, and occasional glimpses of a colorful redbud or white dogwood peeking out from the dense woods as they sped past. He shifted again, as if he couldn't quite get comfortable in his seat.

"You okay?" Mark asked, feeling a twinge of concern. "Did we overdo it?" The long pause only worried him more. "Grandpa?"

"This has always been a pretty drive. No matter what time of year it is."

"Yes, sir." But Mark had a feeling his grandfather wasn't thinking about the scenery.

"I'm a lucky old dog. I've spent a lot of years with the woman I love, and I'm so proud of all my children and grandchildren. And the great-grands." Without taking his gaze from the scenery, he nodded. "Damn lucky."

Mark reached across the console to squeeze Sid's shoulder. "Are you feeling all right?"

"Too maudlin for you?" He patted Mark's hand, his familiar smile returning. "Don't worry about me. I just get tired sooner than I used to. My eighties haven't been too kind to me."

"You know I love our time together, but if these trips are getting to be too much for you, we could stay closer to home. Or do something else." Mark returned his hand to the wheel. "It's the time we spend together that matters. Not the activity. I'd be just as happy to come over and watch a game with you."

"I know." Another worrisome pause. "I just wanted to see all this one more time." Mark was about to press him on what had brought on this sudden melancholy mood when Sid sat up straight and pointed through the windshield at the wisp of a gray-and-black cloud just above the horizon. "Is that smoke?"

They crested the hill and Mark spotted a scene that no firefighter wanted to see. Two mangled cars, compressed together, lying at an angle down in the steep slope of the ditch. "There's been an accident."

"Looks like it's a head-on collision. Mark?"

Mark had already punched in 9-1-1 on his phone on the dashboard as he slowed his truck and pulled onto the shoulder of the highway above the wreck. He set his blinkers on and identified himself to the local dispatcher. "This is Mark Taylor. I'm a Kansas City firefighter. I'm on Highway 7 heading northwest out of Truman Lake." He reported the last mile marker he'd seen to give a better location. "I've got a two-vehicle accident. They've rolled into the ditch. I need fire and a bus to roll ASAP. I'm off duty and don't have all my gear with me, but I'll do what I can to help."

With the promise to notify the local sheriff's office and volunteer firefighters, the dispatcher ended the call. Mark slipped on his black KCFD ball cap, grabbed his phone off its mount and slid out of the truck. "Stay put." But Sid was already climbing out of the other side. "Grandpa."

His grandfather waved him closer. "Hand me your phone. I'll stay out of your way, but the least I can do is watch for traffic and call Dispatch while you work with the victims down there."

Yeah. Even at eighty-seven, this man was a Taylor, born and raised to serve and protect.

Mark winked and handed over the phone. "You know how the fancy new tech works, Grandpa?"

"Get out of here."

Matching the old man's grin, Mark turned down the steep slope, half sliding on the wet grass and half sinking into the water-soaked ditch as he followed the swath of muddy tire tracks down to the two cars.

A quick assessment showed him three potential victims—the teenage boy driving the rusting farm pickup truck, the woman slumped over the steering wheel and deflated airbag of her SUV, and the crying infant strapped into the back seat. With no skid marks on the road above them, he'd wager that one of the drivers had fallen asleep and drifted over the center line. Or one or both drivers had been distracted with a text or phone call. It wasn't his business to determine the cause of the accident or who was responsible—Mark's job was to get everybody out of the wreck alive, treat any injuries and get them safely onto an ambulance or to a hospital for any further care they might need.

Ignoring the mud and water at the bottom of the ditch that oozed up over his hiking boots and soaked into his jeans, Mark reached the SUV first. It was tipped partially onto its side, and he had to climb up onto the running board to see inside. The woman was out cold. Judging by the lump on her forehead and blood dripping from the wound, she'd hit her head on the side window when the vehicles had rolled. With the doors locked, he couldn't check her pulse, but her chest rose and fell, indicating she was still breathing. The car seat in the back was strapped in correctly, and the baby was wailing up a storm, probably good indications that the infant might be scared but hadn't been harmed in the accident.

Mark jumped down and circled around to the driver's side of the pickup. It was partially wedged beneath the SUV and sunk into the mud, and this time he had to squat down to get a look at the driver. The truck was old enough that, without air-conditioning, the kid had been driving with his windows down. Thank God the driver was wearing his seat belt. But he was bleeding from a head wound, too, and holding his chest as he squirmed in his seat, shouting for his phone.

"Where's my phone? I can't find my phone."

"Hey." The startled teen spun toward Mark, wincing with pain. "My name's Mark. I'm here to help you. What's your name?"

"Wyatt," he answered in a breathy gasp. "I can't find my phone. I think it flew out of the truck. I just got it with my last paycheck."

"Okay, Wyatt." Mark kept his tone calm and friendly as he reached inside and turned off the ignition. "I'll look for your phone in a minute. Are you hurt? Do you feel pain anywhere?"

The young man clutched at his chest. "I'm having a hard time catching my breath." That could mean a dozen things, from having the wind knocked out of him to internal injuries. The kid's unfocused gaze might mean a head injury, or he could be going into shock. Mark placed his fingers at the side of his neck. His pulse was fast, but even. That was a good sign, at least. "I'm not sure what happened. Can I get out now? I want to look for my phone. My mom's gonna kill me if I lose another one."

When he opened his dented door, Mark pushed back. Typically, he didn't want the patient moving until he'd done a thorough assessment and had a backboard to put him on. But Mark's eyes and sinuses stung with a whole new set of priorities, as smoke filtered from under the dashboard and through the vents. The same smoke Sid had pointed out earlier. Engine fire.

Mark pulled the door open himself and stood, keeping his voice calm, despite conveying a deep sense of urgency. "Yeah, Wyatt. That sounds like a good idea." The young man unfastened his seat belt and swung his legs out the side of the truck. Mark hooked his arm beneath the young man's shoulders. "Can you stand okay?"

The young man swayed for a moment before smiling from ear to ear. "There it is!"

He reached down and pulled his cell phone from beneath the driver's seat. Mark shook his head and pulled the kid into step beside him, leading him back up the side of the ditch to the shoulder of the road. Another car with an older couple had stopped on the far side of the road. While the woman talked on her phone, hopefully to emergency services, the man had been chatting with Sid. "My wife is talking to the highway patrol. I have a blanket in my car," he offered.

"Get it," Mark ordered. "Grandpa, we need the sleeping bags out of the camper." While the two older men left to fetch those items, Mark did a preliminary exam of Wyatt's head wound. Wyatt's relief might just be fueling him with adrenaline for the moment. He wasn't going to take a chance with the kid going into shock. He sat the young man down and told him to call his parents while the other man wrapped the blanket around his shoulders.

His grandfather dropped the sleeping bags beside Mark. Mark stood, turning over Wyatt's care to the other couple. Sid rubbed his shoulder, as if the joint was stiff from the exertion, and nodded toward the wreckage. "The fire's spreading."

Flames were visible now, shooting through the gaps in the warped hood of the truck and traveling up to the SUV's engine.

"Can you make it down the hill?" Mark asked, jogging to the back of his truck and climbing into the camper. On the fire engine, he'd have a Slim Jim to slide into the SUV's door panel to unlock it. He jumped back down to the pavement. Today, the crowbar from his toolbox would have to do.

"Of course I can. What do you need?" Shaking off Mark's guiding hand, Sid followed him down the slope to the upended SUV.

Mark climbed onto the running board again to peer inside. The woman was conscious now—disoriented, but aware that she and her child were in danger. "Courtney?" She flopped her right arm over the back of the seat. "Are you okay, sweetie? Mommy's here."

Mark knocked on the window, capturing her attention. "Ma'am? I need you to turn off your engine." With a nod of understanding, she turned the key, killing any sparks in the motor that could set off an explosion and turn the small fire into a deadly inferno. Mark held up the crowbar, indicating his intention. "I need you to look the other way."

She turned, raising her hand as if it might shield her baby in the back seat. Mark found the precise spot on the window, shielded his own eyes and shattered the glass with a single blow. In a matter of seconds, he swept the glass shards from the ledge of the door and reached inside to unlock all of them.

"Hang tight, ma'am. I'll be right back."

"Save my little girl," the woman pleaded, understanding Mark's intention as he opened the back door and reached inside. "Is she hurt? It all happened so fast."

"You okay, little one?" A quick check indicated that the car seat had done its job protecting its occupant. Possibly a few bruises, and the child was good and scared, but she quieted and reached for Mark as he inched inside to release the carrier from the car seat. "I think she's okay." He climbed out and handed the baby in her carrier to Sid. "Can you get her up the hill?"

Sid nodded and climbed slowly up the hill. "You come with me, sweetie. I know all about little girls. I have one named Jess. She's a big girl now. But she'll always be my…"

The familiar voice faded as Mark turned his attention to the injured mother. With the seat belt jammed, he pulled out his pocketknife and cut through the straps, catching her before she could slide to the other side of the car. Pulling her arm around his shoulders, he carefully lifted her as he stepped to the ground. Her soft grunt of pain and lack of complaining told him she was probably the more seriously injured of the two drivers. And even though moving her risked aggravating any spinal injury, the spreading flames weren't giving him any choice.

He slid once in the grass, before finding traction and completing the climb. Sid had spread one of the sleeping bags out on the ground where Mark laid the woman. He asked the other woman to hold her hand and talk to her while Sid covered her with the other sleeping bag and set the baby carrier beside her. "There you go, sweetie. There's Mama."

The sounds of distant sirens echoed through the hills as Mark ran to the back of his camper again, pulling out the small fire extinguisher he carried, and dropped back down into the ditch. The pickup's hood was too hot to touch, but it had twisted enough that he could spray the fire-suppressant foam through the gaps and douse the fire. He wouldn't have enough foam to put out two engine fires, but if he could stop the flames from spreading to oil lines and fuel tanks—

"Hey! Mister!" Mark squinted against the stinging chemical fumes of the smoke and ignored the voices calling out.

"Mister Mark! Hey, Firefighter Guy!" That was Wyatt. He turned toward the teen's panicked tone. "He doesn't look too good."

Mark followed his gaze past the two women and baby to where the other man was helping Sid move from his knees, where he'd apparently collapsed, to a sitting position. "Grandpa!"

Sid Taylor was lying flat on his back on the shoulder of the road by the time Mark reached him. Ah, hell. He was pale. His skin was clammy. The subtle signs had been there, but Mark hadn't been paying close enough attention. The pulse at his neck was thready at best.

His grandfather was having a heart attack.

"I'm feeling a little light-headed." Sid's dark eyes drifted shut. "That climb…too much…"

"I shouldn't have asked you to do it. Damn it, I shouldn't have asked." Mark dug through the front pockets of his grandfather's jeans, pulling out the small bottle of baby aspirin. His fingers shook as he twisted it open. This shouldn't be happening. They were supposed to be having fun this weekend. He and Grandpa Sid always had fun.

"Nonsense… Happy to…" For one frightening moment, his voice drifted off.

"Grandpa!" Mark bent his ear to his grandfather's nose and mouth. Was he still breathing? He flattened his palm over Sid's chest, searching for a heartbeat. Where the hell was his med kit when he needed it? Back at the station, on the truck, where it was supposed to be. He and Sid were on vacation. This wasn't supposed to happen. "Grandpa, you hang in there."

After three compressions, Sid's eyes slowly opened. But they were hazy, unable to focus.

"There you are." Mark popped the pill onto Sid's tongue, lifting him slightly and running his hand along his throat to help him swallow. "You scared me, old man. Here. Take this."

Then he laid him flat on the pavement again and resumed compressions.

Someone covered Sid with a blanket. Someone was talking on the phone to 9-1-1. Someone else was crying.

"Did we save the day?" He'd never heard that voice sound so weak.

"Yeah. We sure did, Grandpa." Mark swiped angrily at the tears that clouded his vision. "As soon as the ambulance gets here, they'll all be okay. So will you."

With a flop, Sid covered Mark's hands with one of his, brushing his fingers against Mark's wrist. His touch was cold, jerky. "My good boy. Good…man…"

Sid Taylor's eyes focused for a split second. And then they closed.

"No!" Mark continued the compressions against the old man's brave heart. "Grandpa!"

Chapter Two

Two months later

"What is wrong with you?"

Mark shied away from his brother Alex's flick on the ear, dragged himself from the gloom and guilt of his thoughts, and frowned at his oldest brother's reprimand. "What's wrong with *you*?"

Not the whippiest comeback, but it was the best he could do under the circumstances. Parked on the street in front of the empty butcher shop their grandfather had run for almost fifty years, Mark set the box he'd carried down from his grandmother's apartment above the shop on the tailgate of his truck.

Before he could push it into the bed of the truck, Alex picked up the box and carried it to the pickup parked in front of Mark's, where his brothers Matt and Pike were tying down a dining room table and matching chairs. "That's the third full box of Grandma's things you've tried to load in the back of your truck. Her things go into Matt's truck to haul out to the new house. Grandpa's things go into your truck so we can put them into storage."

Alex might be the shortest of the four Taylor brothers—all adopted into the Taylor clan when they were kids—but there was no doubting his position as the oldest. And possibly the toughest, given his early years as a gang member on the streets of Kansas City. Finding a family like the Taylors, who'd embraced each of them despite their rotten childhoods and the emotional needs they came with, had been a real blessing. They all loved their parents, Gideon and Meghan, as well as their extended family. Brought together first in a foster home and then by adoption, they loved each other, too—and would fight to the death any outsider who threatened their family. But they were still brothers—and picking on the youngest had evolved into an art form over the years.

Probably why Mark had learned at a young age never to back down from standing up for himself and expressing his own opinion. He pulled a black bandanna from the back pocket of his jeans and wiped away the perspiration trickling down his neck before tying it around his forehead to keep the sweat there from running into his eyes. The early summer morning had turned into a long, hot afternoon as it was all hands on deck to help their widowed grandmother move into a ranch-style home with no stairs.

Mark rested his hip against the tailgate. "It doesn't bother you that we're putting Grandpa Sid into storage?"

"It does," Alex agreed, his dark brown eyes a mix of sympathy and reprimand. He stepped aside while brawny Matt pulled a cooler from the back of his truck and opened it to share some iced-down bottles of water. "But we're here to help Grandma today. Moving her to a new place where she doesn't have to climb twenty steps just to get to the front door. Downsizing. Clearing out the apartment so that we can fix it up and she can sell it along with the butcher shop." He tossed Mark a bottle of water and opened one of his own. "She's the one who got left behind, little bro. She needs us to suck up whatever hurt we're feeling and help her get through this." As a SWAT cop, Alex was used to giving orders and expecting them to be obeyed. But he understood that he couldn't just order Mark to stop feeling the grief that distracted him today. "Pike, you're the logical one. Explain this to our baby brother."

The tallest of them, and the only one with blond hair, Edison "Pike" Taylor levered himself off the back of Matt's truck and grabbed one of the water bottles for himself. His KCPD K-9 partner, Hans, was upstairs with his wife and two young children supervising the packing and distracting Martha Taylor from the sadness of the day. "Don't put me in the middle of this.

We all miss Grandpa. I've got a little girl who's never going to know how much her great-grandpa would have spoiled her." He rested an elbow on Alex's shoulder, a long-ingrained habit that reminded their oldest brother that he wasn't the boss here, and that, despite his best intentions, he didn't have all the answers. "Mark was there when we lost him. Maybe that makes it harder for him to compartmentalize and move past it."

Maybe it did.

Mark had saved every life that day except for the one who really counted.

His KCFD counselor kept reminding him to focus on the positive when he got stuck in his head like this. *"Try telling that to the parents of that teenage boy—to the husband and father of that mother and baby."*

"Try telling that to my grandmother. Or parents. Or brothers." Try explaining how he'd let Sid Taylor, the patriarch of this large, wonderful family who'd rescued him, die on the side of the road in the middle of nowhere.

"Hey." The truck shifted as Matt sat on the tailgate beside him. "Get out of your head. This is not your fault."

"Yeah? Just like the death of our birth parents wasn't *your* fault." The shock that flared in Matt's brown eyes was hidden away as quickly as it had appeared. Mark shook his head in apology, hating the way the words had come out of his mouth. He knew the pain his older brother carried. "Hey, man—I'm sorry. That was a low blow. You were a little kid—not even in school yet. No one blames you. Hell, you saved my life that night. It's just…" Mark shrugged. "I know you've struggled with that. When you figure out how to let that one go, you let me in on the secret, okay?"

Matt's gaze narrowed with a considering look. Then he threw an arm around Mark's shoulders and hauled him in for a tight, quick hug. Then he was pushing Mark away and rising to his feet. Ever a man of few words, Matt finished off his water, crumpled the bottle in his fist and went back to his truck. The four brothers packed the remaining boxes into their respective vehicles and headed up the inside stairs to their grandmother's apartment for the next load.

After another hour of packing, they sat down on folding chairs and the floor to share one last Sunday dinner at their grandparents' home. Mark had never left this place hungry, and today was no different. He wolfed down two helpings of potato salad and deli sandwiches, along with samples from the last batch of chocolate chip cookies Grandma Martha would ever bake in this home, where she'd lived with Grandpa Sid for almost fifty years. Somewhere along the way, Mark's mood lightened as his dad and grandmother shared family stories. Hans accepted the offering of a roast beef sandwich from Pike's son to several "Oops" and "Oh, no"s and quick corrections for both dog and boy. And Alex and his wife, Audrey, announced they were taking a class to get certified to adopt a child, which generated a round of hugs and congratulations. Mark wrestled his dad for the last cookie before discovering smarty-pants Pike had already eaten it. Then there was a round of cheers and applause when Grandma Martha pulled a plastic container filled with more cookies from a secret stash in one of the boxes.

Mark was finally laughing when his phone vibrated in the pocket of his jeans. The noise in the big apartment quieted as other phones buzzed or rang with incoming calls and texts. His mother, Meghan, a station captain; his father, an arson investigator and deputy fire chief; as well as his brother Matt—all firefighters—got the same page on their phones.

"Looks like Station 13 needs backup," Mark reported. "They're calling in all off-duty personnel who weren't on the last shift."

"Must be something big," Alex observed.

"I got the same message from my firehouse." Their mother swung her long blond braid behind her back, shifting into command mode as she shared the gist of the message while Mark read the all-call on his phone. Meghan Taylor might be diminutive in size compared to her husband

and the four sons they'd adopted, but as the ranking KCFD officer, Mark and Matt automatically deferred to her. "Looks like volunteer firefighters in Platte County have lost control of a wildfire up north. The winds have shifted and pushed it into our jurisdiction. They thought they had it contained to the brushland and trees, but it's threatening a new housing development and farm homes close to the airport."

Their father, Gideon, was already putting his phone to his ear and striding out of the room. "I'll put in a call to the city—see if we can get some water trucks up there."

Meghan crossed the room to her white-haired mother-in-law. "Martha, I don't want to leave you here. I know this is a tough day for you."

"I'll be just fine, Mcg." Martha Taylor might have lost some height and gained some arthritis over the past few years, but nothing could diminish her innate strength or the bright warmth in her blue eyes. She cupped Meghan's cheek and smiled. "I was married to a marine. And we raised enough cops and firefighters to know that when duty calls, you answer. Don't you worry about me."

Alex slipped his arm around their grandmother's thinning frame. "Audrey and I will stay with her, Mom."

Pike draped an arm around Martha from the

opposite side. "Hope and me and the kids, too. Grandma won't be alone."

Martha reached up and squeezed both Alex's and Pike's hands where they rested on her shoulders, and Mark suspected she was finding the comfort she needed to ease today's abrupt departure as she leaned first into one grandson and then the other. "I never have been. Go. It's because of this family that I have always felt safe."

Meghan nodded and the two women exchanged a hug and a kiss on the cheek. "Love you."

"Love you, too, dear."

Then Meghan turned to Mark and Matt. "Boys?"

Mark imagined they could be sixty, seventy, eighty years old, and their mother would always summon them with *Boys*. Mark didn't mind. He knew he was a lucky son of a gun to be included in this family. Alex, Pike, Matt and he were the boys that, because of a tragic event early in Meghan's life, she'd never been able to have. To his way of thinking, it made the bond between them that much more special because she and Gideon had chosen the four of them to be their boys.

Their father strode back into the room. "The tankers are on their way." He grasped their mother's hand. "Shall we?" He nodded to Mark and Matt. "Why don't you boys drive separately? It sounds like we might need to spread out our resources."

"Yes, sir." Matt swallowed Martha up in a hug

against his broad chest and dropped a kiss on the crown of her hair. "Love you, Grandma."

"Love you, too, Matthew. Be safe."

Her blue eyes locked on to Mark's across the room. Were they sad? Troubled? Or was that the reflection of his own thoughts he saw there? "I love you, too, Mark."

He was the one who'd made this day necessary. How could she say she loved him when he'd taken the love of her life from her?

But her outstretched arms demanded he obey Alex's directive and *suck it up* to do whatever was necessary to ease their grandmother's pain. After the unfamiliar hesitation, he crossed the room and leaned down to wrap her up in a gentle hug. Her slight frame was surprisingly strong as she held on a little longer than he'd planned. "You keep your head in the game and be safe," she whispered against his ear. "I'll be all right."

He didn't deserve her kindness or forgiveness or whatever this was. Still, he tightened his arms as much as he dared because, with everything else she had to deal with right now, he didn't want to add to her burden. "You'd better be," he whispered back before pulling away. "I love you, Grandma."

Then he was jogging down the stairs, following Matt and his parents to their respective vehicles, answering the call for off-duty personnel to provide backup for the exhausted firefighters in North Kansas City.

It was time to go to work.

Time to make sure nobody else died on his watch.

Chapter Three

"Mr. O'Brien, if you could just sign—"

"Do you see how close that fire came to my model home?" Dale O'Brien ignored his assistant, who tried to push a pen and notebook with a page of typed checks toward the contractor, who was building new homes in the area at the edge of the wildfire they'd finally put out. With a heavy sigh that bespoke too little appreciation on too long a day, she hugged the notebook back to her chest and followed her boss as he approached Mark's mom, the local scene commander. Mark watched from his perch on top of the Firehouse 13 truck as the contractor pointed a stubby finger at Meghan Taylor. "I have two buyers who are ready to move into their houses, and eight more lots sold. I have a substantial investment here." O'Brien, the owner of the Copper Lake subdivision near the KCI Airport, had a right to be concerned about the safety of his construction employees and damage to the property he owned.

But a faint accusation laced the tone of the man with a gut pushing over the top of his belt buckle. O'Brien insisted on pointing out the negative instead of focusing on how Mark, Matt and the rest of the KCFD off-duty volunteers who'd answered the call for backup had cleared a trench through the neighboring farmland and watered down a protective perimeter around the new subdivision so that not one of O'Brien's fancy Copper Lake homes and construction sites had sustained any damage from the approaching grass fire.

While Matt was driving the bulldozer they'd used back onto its trailer, Mark and the other firefighters rolled up hoses and stowed their gear in the engine behind his mom. The firefighters were hot, sweaty and grimy, while O'Brien looked like he'd just stepped out of his air-conditioned trailer. He pointed to the charred shell of a tiny house on the far side of the lake that gave the subdivision its name. "This is the third fire we've had out here in less than two months. That's bad for my business. I know it's putting a burden on taxpayers and the KCFD to deal with them. But I don't know what we would have done without your help, Chief Taylor. Clearly, the local yokels can't handle it. Something needs to be done to stop them."

Meghan Taylor pulled off her white helmet and brushed aside the sooty blond curls that stuck to her freckled cheek. "It's Captain, not Chief,

Mr. O'Brien. The county volunteers have been working their butts off to keep these brush fires in check. This one was in danger of jumping the interstate and causing a whole slew of new problems like impaired visibility and traffic accidents. Not to mention encroaching on airport land." Just as he had been for as long as he could remember, Mark was amazed at how tough his mother was. He'd learned long ago not to be fooled by her youthful beauty and soft tone. If Dale O'Brien didn't stop telling her how to do her job, he would soon learn that her gentle demeanor hid a backbone of steel. "You should be thanking them, not insulting them."

"Well, I didn't mean anything by it, of course." He pulled off his hard hat and scratched at his receding hairline before he came up with a new angle that sounded more concerned citizen than whiny businessman. "I was just thinking of the welfare of my men—and your people, too. I know you put lives before property, and that's as it should be. But I don't want Copper Lake to be a frequent call for you."

Mark thought the guy seemed too friendly, too eager to show that this neighborhood was his moneymaker and that he was the big cheese around here. And if he kept pointing that arrogant finger at Mark's mother, Mark was going to break it.

"Mr. O'Brien, please," his young brunette assistant pleaded. "I need to get back to the city and run some errands before my date tonight." She nodded over her shoulder to the pair of men waiting at a beat-up blue sedan near O'Brien's office trailer. While one man lounged on the hood of the car, watching the firefighters work, the other paced beside the car, more focused on the conversation between O'Brien and Mark's mother. "You promised Brad and Richie a paycheck today."

"Can't you see I'm busy, Lissette?" the portly man snapped.

This time, Lissette's sigh held a hint of impatience as she shoved the checks into his chest. "If you want me to work a miracle and make the books balance this month, then you need to pay them. Everyone else gets direct deposit, but you insisted that those two get paid out of petty cash. I won't be responsible for any shortfalls this month. You have to sign."

"Fine." He grabbed the pen, glared at the two men who were now watching intently for his response, then scribbled a line across the bottom of each check. He shoved the notebook back to the young woman and dismissed her. "Tell them they don't need to report for work again until I call them. That'll be all."

"Yes, sir."

Mark watched her hurry over to the two lookie-loos and hand them their checks. The two men made an effort to chat her up after thanking her for getting them paid, but she waved aside their thanks and hurried into the office trailer to deposit the notebook and retrieve her purse before quickly driving away.

The rest of O'Brien's men—the ones not getting paid out of petty cash—had packed up their work trucks. Maybe those two had been waiting around for the chance to get a few more hours in on their paychecks once KCFD cleared the scene. But with black smoke still coiling across the horizon, gusting winds threatening to reignite fires, and some of the access roads into the farm country and public woodlands blocked by firefighting equipment and crew vehicles, he didn't anticipate anyone getting back to work before the next morning.

Once the hose was secured, Mark slid down the ladder at the back of the Lucky 13 truck and grabbed his turnout coat and helmet. Instead of heading to his truck, he lingered to hear a little more of the conversation the contractor insisted on having with the captain.

"I warned my crew about smoking in the dry grass," O'Brien announced. "And to police the sparks from their power tools. They're supposed to work over a paved area or the dirt. But I can't keep my eye on them 24/7. Nothing out here a good rainstorm wouldn't cure. An end to this drought would make life a lot easier for all of us."

Meghan Taylor shook her head. "These fires

didn't start where your men are working. The fires are coming from the other direction, across the lake where that farmland is. The wind is what moved the fire toward your property."

Mark scanned the far side of the lake as O'Brien pointed across the water to the hilly landscape. "A lot of that is my land, too. Or will be. The landowner, Mrs. Hall, is selling it off in chunks as we build the new homes out here. She's a widow now and getting on in years, can't keep up with it all. I expect when she's ready to move into the city and sell off the rest of it—I mean, it's not like she's farming it herself—I'll own the property around the entire lake. We're building quite a nice bedroom community out here. Quality homes with an easy commute into downtown."

Mark knew that his mom wasn't interested in O'Brien's sales pitch. She pointed to the empty lots beyond the newly built model home and the two houses that were already under construction on either side of the street. "You've got all the proper permits here? There's only one hydrant on the north side of the lake."

"The city hasn't repaved the street and updated the water main there yet. Those houses are on well water." Had O'Brien dodged the question about permits? Or was he still intent on impressing Mark's mom with his grandiose plans? "Once I tear them down and build new homes, the view to the north will improve one hundred percent."

Mark eyed the dilapidated string of houses on the far side of the lake. Besides the burned one, another had a listing boat dock, making those homes look like the poor neighbors of O'Brien's fancy new lakeside community. Only one of the tiny houses had a decent roof. The farmhouse at the top of the rise beyond them looked in better shape. But that might be deceptive since the front of the house was camouflaged by scaffolding. It was painted an antique white about halfway down the shingled siding of the two-story colonial, while the bottom half just looked antique, as in peeling, warped and faded. But the roof was new, a shiny warm corrugated copper that gleamed with the orange-red glow of the late summer sun. And the whole thing sat in a patch of green grass, an indicator that the homeowner cared more about the property than O'Brien claimed. Not only was the old woman fixing up the house, but she had watered the yard more frequently than any of the newly sodded properties O'Brien had built.

"I just want to know that my men are safe out here," O'Brien added. "And that they can get back to work sooner rather than later. Idle time is wasted money."

About the time Mark decided to interrupt the conversation to tell O'Brien to clear out with the last of his men, and give his mom an excuse for ending the stocky man's gripe-and-brag session, the door to the farmhouse flew open and a woman ran out.

Even if he hadn't heard the slap of the door slamming shut behind her, he couldn't have missed the flag of a copper-red ponytail flying out behind her as she ran to an old blue-and-white pickup parked in the gravel driveway. Although he couldn't make out the details of her face, the stretch of long legs between khaki shorts and hiking boots pounding down the steps and front walk screamed that something was wrong. The hackles on the back of Mark's neck went up another notch as she executed a quick three-point turn and gunned the engine, racing down the driveway toward the weathered asphalt that separated the farmhouse from the run-down lakeside buildings.

"What the hell?"

Mark was already skirting around his mom and Mr. O'Brien when the woman made a sharp left turn onto another gravel road, churning up a cloud of dust in her wake as she crested the hill and headed down the other side. Speeding her way north. Away from the subdivision. Away from the lake and the farmhouse.

Driving *toward* the brush fire.

His mom flanked him for a moment, both watching as the woman headed straight toward the danger they'd worked so hard to avert. Meghan Taylor turned her head to the radio clipped to her turnout coat and asked for a sit-rep, a situation report. "Were all civilians evacuated from the area north of the lake?" She turned back to Dale O'Brien. "Do you know who that young woman is?"

He chuckled. "Crazy Amy. She lives there with her grandma."

"Do you have a last name for her? Contact information?"

Mr. O'Brien shrugged. "In my trailer. I've got the home number for her grandmother's house in my phone."

"I need that." She tilted her brown eyes to Mark. "We have to stop her. I'll work on calling her and get over to the house to make sure the grandmother isn't still inside. You—"

"I'm on it, Captain." Mark ran to his truck and tossed his helmet and turnout coat inside before climbing in.

But a large hand clamped around the edge of the door, preventing him from closing it. Big brother Matt had a habit of showing up without announcing himself. "Where do you think you're going?"

Mark started the engine. "After that woman. She's driving straight into wildfire territory instead of away from it like anyone with a lick of sense would." When Matt's suspicious glare didn't so much as blink, Mark grumbled a curse under his breath, knowing what his brother must be thinking after their conversation earlier that day. "I don't have a death wish. But I think maybe she does."

"You don't have to save everybody."

This wasn't about Grandpa Sid and the guilt he felt. "I'm doing my job, Matt."

Matt arched a questioning eyebrow, but this wasn't the time to psychoanalyze him. It was time to act. "Make sure that's all it is." He closed the door, but he didn't release it. "Want me to go with you?"

Mark looked beyond him to see O'Brien futzing with his phone, while their mother waited for the promised phone number. "No. Stay with Mom. I can't tell if that O'Brien guy is up to something, or if he's worried about his investments burning down out here. He sure as hell has no clue how to talk to a lady. I know she can handle herself, but—"

"She's our mom. I'm on it." Matt shoved his hand through the open window to trade a fist bump with Mark. "Eyes open, bro. Keep us apprised of your twenty."

Mark tapped his fist against Matt's, understanding the friendly warning to stay aware of any shift in the winds kindling a new fire or catching behind him and cutting him off from his escape. "Will do."

Mark shifted into Drive and took off, reassured to see Matt joining their mother and Mr. O'Brien in his rearview mirror. By the time he'd left the new pavement and circled around the lake, he'd lost sight of the red-haired woman. But there weren't that many places she could go out here, were there?

He turned off the asphalt, pressing a little harder than he probably should on the gravel surface. After fishtailing around the turn, he crested the road she had taken, and discovered the remains of what had once been a working farm. He passed an old horse paddock with charred broken railings and a stable whose roof had partially collapsed in on its brick walls. The blackened studs and surviving beams at one end indicated the fire in the paddock had climbed the exterior walls and taken down the roof. Idly, he wondered if the fires had caused the property on this side of the lake to look run-down and abandoned— or if abandoning the farming and caring for the structures had led to the fires.

But it wasn't all run-down. Beyond the stable was an equipment shed that was built in a similar design. The barn wood had a fresh coat of white paint on it, a new corrugated metal roof that matched the house, and a padlocked door. Clearly, that building was still in use, but the padlock on the outside told him the mysterious redhead hadn't gone in there.

Mark looked ahead to the rolling hills that had gone wild with brittle brown prairie grass and scrub pines that dotted the sea of brown with tufts of green. A row of charred fence posts swept over the hills like a gothic version of holiday garland. Nothing he could see was tall enough to give shelter or hide the redhead's truck. He looked to his left to see the undulating line of black crossing the nearest hilltop, indicating the line the fire had reached before the winds had moved the flames in another direction. He spotted the flames climbing the next hill, and the team of volunteer firefighters spaced along the front line to keep it from advancing. While the trench his own team had dug, and the lake itself, would protect the subdivision for now, that farmhouse and the buildings on the north side of the lake were still vulnerable. Anything between the lake and the natural firebreak of paved and gravel roads to the north and west was still vulnerable to the mercurial path of the fire.

And that woman with the striking copper hair had driven right into the heart of it.

A wary alertness pricked the nape of Mark's neck as he discovered a crossroads at the base of the next hill. He didn't have eyes on her yet, but Mark didn't hesitate to turn left. The dry earth formed a plume of dust behind her truck that was as easy to spot as the woman's red ponytail.

"Finally." He spotted the dust cloud settling around the blue-and-white pickup near a burned-out bridge over a narrow creek. The woman had stopped at the roadblock warning drivers to steer clear of the wildfire area. Mark skidded to a stop behind her battered truck. But as their cumulative dust cloud drifted past him, he saw that she was out of the truck, climbing over the barricade. When her hiking boots hit the charred grass on the opposite side, she took off running again.

Even though his truck could handle a little off-roading, with no clear line of sight to determine the current location of the fire, Mark couldn't risk driving after her. In seconds, he was out of his truck, swearing at her persistence and chasing after her. "Hey! Lady, stop!"

If anything, those long legs of hers picked up speed as she climbed up the opposite side of the embankment. Mark swore. Either she was deaf, purposely ignoring him or actually *was* crazy, like O'Brien had said.

Although he'd stripped down to his T-shirt and suspenders in deference to the heat, Mark still wore his bunker pants and boots. Their heavy, protective weight was necessary for fighting fires, but not the best gear for a cross-country race. But Crazy Amy's reckless charge left him little choice but to go after her. Lengthening his own strides, he climbed the bank of the creek and closed the gap between them.

"Ma'am?" he shouted. He was close enough to hear her labored breathing now. She'd been running hard. Or maybe the stranger chasing her down had panicked her. "I'm KCFD. I don't mean to frighten you, but you're entering dangerous territory. I need you to stop and come with me."

"I can't." She stumbled over the slick mix of dirt and ash, swore at her clumsiness and relentlessly pushed herself back to her feet.

But her tumble slowed her enough for Mark to reach her. He caught hold of her arm beneath the rolled-up sleeve of her blouse, abruptly stopping her ascent and pulling her around to face him. "I believe I'm the authority here."

She shoved long coppery bangs off her face, leaving a streak of soot on her freckled cheek. "I believe this is my land. Well, my gran's." She made a fussy noise and twisted her elbow from his grip before lunging up the hill again. "I'm sorry. I can't talk to you right now."

"Can't…?" In two long strides he was in front of her, holding out his hands, hoping to calm down this flight response and reason with her. "My name is Mark Taylor." He pulled aside one strap of his suspenders and pointed to the logo on his T-shirt. "I'm with the Kansas City Fire Department."

"Good for you." She darted around him.

"Hey!" This time he grabbed her with both hands, keeping a firm grip on each upper arm. A unique pendant, which looked like a knotted rope of silver, rose and fell with every breath against the freckles dotting her ample chest above the tank top she wore beneath her blouse. But the shiny metal wasn't nearly as bright as the gold flecks sparking against the green irises of her eyes. He glanced over his shoulder, thinking maybe that was the encroaching fire he saw flickering there. But no, she was just pissed that he'd outmuscled her for her own good. Easing his grip on her, and taking a deep breath to calm his demeanor, Mark explained the danger so she would understand his concern. "KCFD and the Platte County Volunteer Fire Department has the fire contained for now. But it covers acres, miles, maybe. And it's still burning. Plus, the way this wind is blowing, we don't know if it will stay contained or head back this way."

Mark was six-two, and even though he stood slightly uphill of her, the woman barely tilted her chin to maintain eye contact with him. That height explained the mile-long legs. "Thank you for that PSA, Mark Taylor, but I'm willing to risk it." She waved her hand as though she was shooing him away, flashing a variety of chunky rings on her thumb and fingers. "I absolve you of responsibility. Be gone with you."

She scooted around him again.

"Be gone with…?" Had he slipped into some universe populated by flakes and stubborn women who wouldn't listen? He grabbed her one more time, pulling her closer to his body so she couldn't twist away. That didn't stop her from pushing at his chest and trying. "You're nuts, lady. I'm trying to rescue you here."

"I don't need you to rescue me!" All at once the air rushed from her lungs and her expression changed. On first glance, he might have thought her unadorned face was rather unremarkable. But those green-gold eyes offered a fascinating glimpse of her emotions. They were darker now, as green as the charred landscape around them should have been. She wasn't crazy. Something was wrong. Seriously wrong. Something clutched inside him as she patted the KCFD logo over his heart. "I need you to help me."

"Help you do what? Get yourself killed?" Her hands settled against his shoulders and he felt her arms stiffen. She was getting ready to bolt again. He calmed his tone, hoping to reason with her. "You're running toward the flames, not to safety."

"Isn't that what you do? Run toward danger?"

"One of us is trained and the other isn't."

She pushed and tried to twist free. The soft, frightened moment had passed. Her eyes were sparking again. "Then be a hero and help me find my friend. She's somewhere out here in the middle of all this."

"I'm no hero." Her description grated against Mark's guilt, but he shoved his feelings aside and worked harder to assess the situation before she escaped again. "I'm just doing my job. Now tell me about your friend, and do not run from me again."

Her arms relaxed their stiff posture and he released her. "Jocelyn Brunt. College roommate. Best friend. She's the yin to my yang. Introvert-extrovert. Scientist-artist—you get the idea. Jocelyn's a researcher, working on her PhD in environmental science. She was working up near the apple trees that run along the eastern property line. She's been living with my gran and me the past couple of semesters."

He noted the direction of her pointing thumb. "The old farmhouse by Copper Lake? Weren't you ordered to evacuate?"

"Of course we were. I drove Gran into the city to stay with one of her friends."

"But Jocelyn didn't go with you?"

"Would I be here if she had?" She gestured to the top of the hill behind him, frustrated with his lack of clairvoyant understanding of her concern. "There are still several old buildings on the property. Jocelyn uses one of the old feed sheds to store her equipment when she's out in the field checking the soil and plant growth, so she doesn't have to haul it back and forth every day. I called her as soon as we were notified the fire had changed course. One of the things she studies is how fire affects different kinds of soil with different kinds of crops or grazing land like this, so I thought maybe she was taking a little extra time to pick up her data. It's my fault I didn't check in with her right away. She said she was on her way to the shed to lock up her stuff, and then she'd join us." The breeze whipped her long bangs across her face again, and Mark squeezed his fingers into a fist, surprised by the instinctive urge to brush the russet waves aside and tuck them behind her ear. "That was six hours ago."

"Did you try calling her again?"

"Of course I did. I'm not an idiot. Her phone goes straight to voice mail." She tilted her nose into the air as the wind shifted. Mark could smell it, too. Smoke. All the more reason to solve this woman's problem and get her out of the fire zone. "She could be trapped out here somewhere. I hoped that she had gone back to the house because you guys stopped the fire, but her Jeep wasn't there. What if she holed up in the shed, thinking that was safe? Or she tried to hike back to the house but got cut off by the fire? You saw that roadblock and the scorch marks on the ground—all the way down to the creek. I'm afraid something has happened to her."

Now he understood. There was another life to save. "Where is this shed?"

"I'll take you."

"No, that's not what I…" But she was already jogging ahead. Mark turned his face to the smoky sky and swore before hurrying after her. He caught her arm and stopped her again.

"Fine. I'll give you fifteen minutes. You lead the way. But if I see anything I don't like, if I think you're in immediate danger, I will order you to stop, and we will leave."

"Fine." She was running again.

Mark clamped his hand over her arm once more and turned her to face him. Her eyes were deep green with emotion now—she was probably pissed at him for being so bossy. But he meant business. He took the time to radio in a sit-rep and give his team an approximate location and their destination before he spoke to the woman again. "What's your name, Red? That O'Brien guy called you Crazy Amy. I don't intend to do that."

"Dale O'Brien is a bully and a prig." She muttered a choice expletive that made Mark wonder what the pudgy contractor had done to her. But that conversation was for another time. And a different man. This was a rescue op, not a get-acquainted date. "I'm Amy Hall."

"All right, Amy Hall. I will help you find your friend. But you do what I tell you, when I tell you, or I will throw you over my shoulder and carry you away from that fire myself. That's the only way we're moving forward."

She seemed to consider just how serious he was about the over-the-shoulder threat—or maybe she was just desperate to end this conversation and get to her friend.

But then she nodded. "I can live with that." She

shifted her grip to lace her fingers together with his and pulled him into a jog behind her. "Let's go, Fire Man."

It was a steeper jog down this hill, and Mark was glad he had a hold of Amy when her feet slipped from underneath her. She didn't complain about the soot mark on the rump of her khaki shorts, but simply thanked him and fell into step beside him again as they climbed to the top of the next hill.

They both halted when they reached the devastation waiting for them there.

"Oh, my God." Amy's hand tightened convulsively around Mark's. Then she released him and ran toward the burned-out shell of a Jeep. "Jocelyn!"

"Hold on."

"Jocelyn!" After a quick circle around the Jeep to inspect its empty interior, Amy dashed over to the carbonized wood planks and metal debris that had once been the feed shed.

Mark spared an extra minute to make sure the fuel lines were secure and there was no gasoline or oil pooling beneath the vehicle that could start another fire.

"Amy!" The wildfire had blazed a trail across the top of the hill, turning everything in its path to ash before moving on. If her friend had taken refuge here, or the flames had moved too quickly for her to escape, she hadn't survived.

There was only one woman he could help now.

Amy lifted a board with her bare hands, and it disintegrated. She lifted the one beneath it and tossed it aside. That board hit the ground and kicked up a cloud of black that could be charcoal dust or smoke. He climbed through the wreckage of the old shed after her. "Amy, stop! There could still be hot spots underneath the debris."

"Jocelyn? Please tell me you were smart enough to get out of..." She spotted something at the bottom of the pile and climbed over some charred chunks of metal he assumed had been Jocelyn's equipment. "Oh, no. Please no."

He saw it, too. The charred remains of a body.

"Amy, stop." Mark pushed Amy behind him and took over clearing the debris around the ghastly skeleton. "We don't know who it is. Someone else could have taken shelter. I need you to stand aside..."

But Amy was kneeling in the area he'd cleared. Her cheeks were pale at first, then flushed with emotion as a tear rolled down her cheek. Mark knelt beside her, intent on pulling her away from the remains.

But once again, Amy Hall refused to do what made sense. She reached down to tug at the blackened chain that had fallen inside the victim's rib cage. Mark draped an arm around her shoulders as she rubbed the soot off the chain's pendant to reveal a glimpse of knotted silver.

"That's just like yours," he whispered.

Amy dropped the necklace and wrapped her fist around the pendant at her own neck. "I made it for her. Jocelyn…" A sob broke free and Amy turned her face into Mark's chest. He wrapped her up in his arms and pulled her to her feet, tucking her face against the juncture of his neck and shoulder and holding her as Amy wept for her friend. "It's her. I'm too late. It's her."

As Mark held on tight, shielding Amy from the gruesome sight, he recognized something, too—scorch marks across and around the body. While his heart grieved for Amy Hall's loss, another, darker emotion welled up inside him.

Anger.

The scorch marks were the pour pattern of an accelerant crisscrossing the corpse, indicating the woman had been doused in some sort of chemical and set on fire—postmortem, he hoped. Burning alive was a hell of a way to die. And if he wasn't mistaken, the dent in Jocelyn Brunt's skull suggested something even more sinister.

Amy's fists gradually eased their death grip at the back of his shirt, but he held on as he walked her away from the dead body. Keeping Amy's face averted from the gruesome scene, Mark reached for his radio and called it in.

This fire was no accident. He needed to in-form the scene commanders that at least part of today's wildfire was the result of arson—a fire deliberately set to cover up the scene of a murder.

Chapter Four

"When was the last time you saw Ms. Brunt?" The female detective with the long brown ponytail and seriously unfriendly frown tapped her phone with her metal stylus. "I mean alive, of course."

While KCFD investigators pored over the burned-out wreckage of Jocelyn's Jeep and the old shed on the north edge of the property, and a medical examiner took her friend's body to the crime lab, KCPD detectives had brought Amy back to the house to take her statement and go through Jocelyn's things.

Amy flicked her gaze over to Detective Cathy Beck's cold green eyes, but quickly dismissed the shorter woman's mood as they stood together inside the doorway to Jocelyn's bedroom. "Early this morning. Breakfast." Nervously fingering the silver knot that hung from the chain around her neck, Amy watched Detective Beck's partner, Dean Carson, toss the bedding. Less than a week ago, she and Jocelyn had sat up all night on that bed, pigging out on coffee ice cream and discussing the mess of their respective love lives and work woes. When the compactly built blond detective left the quilt and pillows in a pile and bent down to study something on the exposed sheet more closely, Amy asked, "What is he doing? He's making a mess of her things. Jocelyn didn't entertain guests here."

Detective Beck tapped something into her phone. "Did she entertain them somewhere else?"

Amy shook her head, closing her fist around her necklace. Jocelyn had kept her room organized and uncluttered. The speed with which the burly detective was destroying all that twisted a knot in her stomach. "She was focused on finishing her PhD," Amy answered. "She was excited about the fires adding a new dimension to her dissertation. All she had left was this semester and orals in the spring."

"So, Ms. Brunt was completely focused on her work." Detective Beck jotted a note on her phone. "Was there a boyfriend—or girlfriend—who felt neglected?"

"She had a boyfriend on and off." A lot of that last late-night ice cream bash had centered around Jocelyn's ex, Derek Roland. Amy shrugged. "But they were *off*. They were doing similar research, and she thought there might be a conflict of interest when it came time to present their findings to the dissertation board."

"Conflict of interest?"

Man, she really did not want to talk about the prejudices and bias that an assistant dean and group of professors could exert over a doctoral student, especially a female one. But she wanted to identify whoever had killed Jocelyn more. Her own experience was water under the bridge now. If answering questions that dredged up those uncomfortable memories was what it took, then she would do it. "Jocelyn was worried the professors might think she'd copied Derek's research. More likely, Derek would have copied hers. She was brilliant and determined, and he was…lazy. Always looking for shortcuts."

"Did Ms. Brunt ask for the time off from their relationship, or did he?"

"Jocelyn suggested they take a break." Amy shivered uncomfortably. These questions felt like she was ratting out someone else she had considered a friend, too. But Derek's charm had worn thin when his demands on Jocelyn's time had made Jocelyn question whether he was interested in her or her research. Amy almost laughed when she considered Derek's aversion to spending endless hours out in the field. Would he literally dirty his hands in the soot and blood of the crime scene? Much less hurt the woman he professed to love? "Until after her orals. He agreed."

Detective Beck's grunt of agreement made Amy wonder if the woman with the badge doubted the mutual decision of Jocelyn's breakup. "Does Derek have a last name?"

Amy spelled out Derek Roland's last name. "He's a doctoral student at Williams University, too."

Detective Carson was pulling open drawers on Jocelyn's dresser now, touching all of her friend's things with his gloved hands. "I've got a box of condoms in here," he announced to his partner before stuffing T-shirts and jewelry back inside. "But I'm not finding any obvious signs of a struggle. No love letters or threatening notes. The only pictures are in that album beside the bed. A lot with the boyfriend." He thumbed over his shoulder as he moved on to the next drawer. "And Ms. Hall there."

"This feels like we're violating her privacy," Amy protested when Detective Carson grabbed a fistful of underwear to look underneath it. "Jocelyn was supersmart, but shy. I'm the one who got into trouble, not her. She was all about studying and work."

Detective Beck touched Amy's shoulder to keep her from crossing the room to halt her partner's search. "Trust me. Getting to know your friend—any secrets, any conflicts, any habits—is the first step in figuring out who wanted to harm her. Especially with as little forensic evidence as we'll get from that crime scene. We'll be as respectful as we can be with her things, but we need to do this."

Amy swallowed her outrage, hugged her arms around her waist and drifted back into the doorway. "I don't know anyone who would want to hurt Jocelyn. None of this makes sense."

"Our job is to help it make sense." Detective Beck's frown faded beneath the hint of a compassionate smile. "Would Ms. Brunt's things be anywhere else in the house?"

"Clothes in the laundry room. Some of her food is in the kitchen. She was a vegetarian. Gran didn't even want to touch her tofu." Amy rubbed her fingers along the rolled-up sleeves of her soiled blouse. Even though she'd washed her hands and splashed cool water on her face to ease the feverish aftermath of her tears, she realized she still wore the grubby, soot-stained clothes she'd had on that afternoon. By the time she'd gotten back to the house, the police had asked to see Jocelyn's room, and she'd had no time to herself from that moment on. "Jocelyn kept the rest of her work stuff in the shed that burned. Or in her car. She carried her life in her backpack, and she always had that with her."

"Where is her backpack now?"

"No sign of it here," Detective Carson confirmed.

Detective Beck tapped herself a note before

looking up at Amy. She could only answer the truth. "I don't know."

Had she seen the backpack at the crime scene? She didn't remember seeing straps around the corpse's shoulders, but maybe even that tough nylon material could have burned to the point of disintegration. She'd like to ask Fire Man Mark if that was a possibility. She wanted to ask him if he thought Jocelyn had suffered before she died, too. She wanted to know if he'd consider wrapping those buff arms of his around her again to make the vision of the devastating scene she'd witnessed recede a little bit again.

Amy was taller than many of the men she knew. She was taller than Detective Carson over there. Her grandfather had always called her a *healthy girl*. And though she was reasonably fit from the training classes she'd taken after her last relationship had ended so badly, no one would ever call her skinny. Still, Mark Taylor had made her feel delicate, feminine, safe. It was probably the whole firefighter/rescuer vibe he gave off. But Amy was used to rescuing herself. Life had trained her to be self-sufficient, not to rely on someone else's love and support to sustain her when the going got tough. She'd forgotten how vulnerable a punch of grief could make her feel. Or how good it felt to not have to be the strong one for a change.

And that whole throw-her-over-his-shoulder

caveman threat had been surprisingly…intriguing. Fire Man Mark hadn't meant anything sexual by it, of course. But some errant hormone deep inside had lit up with interest as if it had been. His words and steely-eyed glare had felt like some kind of dare—and for a split second during her search for Jocelyn, she'd foolishly wanted to call him on it.

Okay, sexy, strong and attractive in a ruggedly masculine way was all well and good for her hormones. But depend on him? That was dangerous thinking.

Accidental death, malicious intent and now murder had ripped away every support system Amy had ever counted on. With the exception of her grandmother, whose age was beginning to shift the balance in that relationship, even, Amy knew better than to put her trust in anyone but herself.

"Did Ms. Brunt keep an office at the university?"

Detective Beck's question pulled Amy from the fruitless turn of her thoughts. Amy nodded. "But Jocelyn never used it. Not when she was out in the field like she was this semester. Everything she needed was in that shed or on her laptop in her backpack."

The dark-haired detective nodded. "All right. We'll make finding that backpack priority one."

Amy's phone rang in the back pocket of her

shorts. Automatically, she pulled it out, despite Detective Beck's apparent impatience at having the interview interrupted. But when Amy saw the name on the screen, her breath tightened in her chest. She knew any other questions would have to wait. "I need to take this call. Is that all right?"

The detective took a break from putting notes into her phone. "Make it quick." Then she nodded past Amy to the uniformed officer waiting in the hallway. "When you're done, would you show the laundry and food items to Officer Marquette?"

"Joss's laptop won't be there."

"I'd like someone to have a look anyway," the detective explained. "We'll check her office at the university, and with the ex-boyfriend, too." Amy's phone burned in her hand. "*Not* finding that laptop, or locating it in an unexpected place, could be as important as finding it."

"I understand. Excuse me." Amy stepped into the hallway and swiped the answer button. With half the upstairs landing draped in paint tarps and the stairwell itself lined with ladders and scaffolding from her remodeling efforts, it was almost impossible to find a private corner to have this conversation. So, she drifted to the railing overlooking the downstairs entryway and dropped her voice to a whisper. "Derek?" How, exactly, was she supposed to start this conversation? It wasn't going to be by announcing that KCPD wanted to talk to him. "Are you sitting down?"

He laughed. "Of course I'm sitting down. I'm driving my car." She could hear another voice in the background, and supposed he had the news on his radio or was listening to a podcast. The background voice suddenly went silent. He must have turned off whatever was playing. "Why are you whispering? I can barely hear you."

"Where are you? I need you to pull off onto a side street or parking lot."

"Are you kidding? I'm halfway to your place on I-29." She heard the change in his tone as he realized she wouldn't have made her request if something wasn't seriously wrong. "What's happened? I called you because I've been trying to get a hold of Joss all afternoon, and she's not picking up. I'm not even getting her voice mail. Is she okay?"

Amy could barely squeeze the word past the tightness in her chest and throat. "No. She's not. There's been...an accident."

Several seconds passed before Derek spoke again. "How badly is she hurt? Are you at the hospital? She didn't get trapped by the fires, did she?"

"Not exactly—"

"She was supposed to evacuate with you. Why didn't you make sure she got back to civilization—"

"Derek." She interrupted him as accusation filled his voice. "Someone killed her."

"What?"

"I discovered the body. The fire was a forensic countermeasure to hide whatever happened to her."

She imagined he drove another mile in silence, or maybe he'd finally pulled off onto the shoulder of the road, before he answered. "She was murdered? Why?"

"That's the question of the day, it seems." Amy wound her fingers around the polished oak railing that framed the landing, needing its solid form to lean on for a moment until she could compose her thoughts. "The police want to talk to you since you and Joss were so close. And because you know about her research, what she might have had on her laptop. Any chance you know where that is?"

"Her laptop? Why would I know that?"

She glanced over her shoulder when she realized both Officer Marquette and Detective Beck had tuned in to her conversation. She turned her back to them, trying to reclaim a little privacy. "Look, I need to wrap this up."

Suddenly, his voice dropped to a whisper to match hers. "Are the cops there right now?"

"Yes."

"Why?"

Why would the police investigate a murder? "They're asking questions. Looking for leads." She exhaled a breath she didn't realize she'd been holding when Detective Carson called Detective

Beck back into the room to look at something. "You can come on out to the house if you want to hang out and commiserate. Or if you want to be with me when I call Jocelyn's parents."

"I can't deal with that right now. I can't deal with any of that."

She moved her hand from the railing to the steel pipe of construction scaffolding that rose above it from the foyer below. The metal felt shockingly cold in her grasp. It had picked up the chill of the air-conditioning, no doubt. Or maybe she was the one who was losing any remnant of warmth.

"I'm turning this car around," Derek announced. "I'll talk to you later, Amy. I need some time alone to process this first."

Man, did she understand that impulse. "Derek, Jocelyn really did care about you."

"Yeah. She cared so much that she didn't want to be with me." Amy didn't know what to say to that. If KCPD saw him as a jilted lover or jealous grad student, would they consider him a suspect? "Don't tell the police I said that. Okay?"

"Okay. But you should tell them."

She heard the extra voice in the background of the call again. He'd turned on whatever he'd been listening to and was tuning her out. "Thanks for giving me the heads-up. Call me if you find out anything else."

"I will. Derek, are you okay to be driving?

Will you call me when you get home, so I know you're safe?"

"Sure. Whatever."

"I'm so sorry to be the one to tell you. I know you must hurt as much as I—"

The call abruptly disconnected. And Amy doubted it had anything to do with a dropped call. Hadn't anger been one of her initial reactions to losing Jocelyn? Why should the man who'd loved her be any different? If Derek didn't contact her later, Amy would call him to make sure he was all right. For now, she'd give him his space to get past the shock and start to grieve. Pulling her hand from the unbending steel that suddenly reminded her of prison bars rising up in front of her, she slowly slipped the phone back into her pocket, inhaled a couple of deep breaths and then gestured to the uniformed officer to follow her down the wide oak stairs.

"The laundry room is this way."

Detective Beck stuck her head out the bedroom door with one last directive for the uniformed officer. "Check any pockets. Signs of trace. You know the drill."

"Yes, ma'am."

"Careful. The stain on that railing might still be tacky." Urging the black woman in the KCPD uniform to stick to the wall on the right side of the stairs, away from the construction scaffolding, Amy led her down to the foyer. The main part of the house, inside and out, felt like a barricaded fortress, with honeycombs of metal framework circling the interior of the two-story entryway and the front of the house so that she and the two workmen she'd hired could repair and refinish the century-old interior oak paneling, as well as repaint the exterior of the old farmhouse. "Watch your head."

Amy ducked beneath the wood planks that formed a squared-off archway between the foyer and the rooms in the back that had already been modernized and repainted after a year and a half of hard work and restoration. While she enjoyed working with her hands and bringing out the beauty of the old home, it had proved to be too big a project to complete on her own. She had her own contracted art pieces to finish, including her metal sculpting and jewelry work. And with Dale O'Brien breathing down her grandmother's neck with monetary offers and subtle threats to drive them off the land he wanted to build on, the need for speed had grown even greater. She planned to turn the house into a historic masterpiece of turn-of-the-century architecture and petition the state and national register of historic places to give her gran's house protected status, preserving the only home her grandmother had ever known and protecting the natural beauty of the land where her great-grandparents had once grown apple trees and raised cattle.

Provided these wildfires—whether accidental or deliberate—didn't burn them out first.

As she straightened on the other side of the arch, she collided with a string bean of a man in faded blue jeans and work boots. Handyman #1, Brad Frick. Brad put his hand out to grab her shoulder to keep them from bumping into each other. "Careful there, Miss Amy. Look out."

"Brad. You startled me." Flattening her palm over the drumming of her heart, Amy offered the construction worker a friendly smile. Brad compensated for the receding points of his hairline by growing a long ponytail that nearly reached his waist in the back. Along with his beakish nose, he'd always reminded her of a long-legged bird—one who'd be easy to sculpt into a humorous garden decoration with the scrap metal and welding equipment she stored in her art studio.

"Hey, Miss Amy." His partner, Richie Sterling, who was changing out the paper on a hand sander on the sawhorses behind him, was too nondescript to spark any obvious artistic inspiration. Richie was average height, average weight and hid his average blond-brown hair beneath a paint-stained ball cap. About the only thing unique about him was the streaks of sunburn that seemed to perpetually stain his cheeks.

She widened her smile to include Richie in her greeting. "Hey, Richie. What are you two doing here?"

"We're w-w-working," he answered, cutting the excess sandpaper off with the blade of a box cutter. His gaze skipped from her to the female officer beside her before dropping to the gun strapped at Officer Marquette's waist. "Is that real?"

Officer Marquette nodded, resting her hand on the butt of the weapon. "Yes, sir. Very much so."

"Do you know how to use it?" Richie asked.

The woman's impassive professional face softened with a smile. "I'd better know how if I'm going to be carrying it."

"Cool." Richie lifted his gaze, although it danced over the other woman's face without making direct eye contact. "Did you ever shoot anyone with—"

"Richie!" Brad chastised his friend. "Back to work."

Nodding at the command, Richie lowered his head to attach a battery pack to the cordless sander.

"Sorry about that, ma'am." Brad turned his attention back to the nail hole he was filling with Spackle. "Sometimes, his curiosity gets the better of him. He's harmless."

Officer Marquette exchanged a quizzical look with Amy at the odd addendum before sharing her smile with Brad, as well. "That's all right, sir. Sometimes, folks are curious about a woman in uniform." The smile was gone when she looked back at Amy. "Ma'am? If you could show me the items you mentioned?"

"Sure."

But the alleged brainy half of Frick and Frack here moved a sawhorse table out of his way so he could move closer to the paneling, effectively blocking Amy and the female officer's path. "The Copper Lake construction site is closed down for the rest of the day because of the fires. I'd hate to lose whatever daylight we have left when we could still put in a couple of hours and make a few bucks." He smoothed the Spackle with his putty knife, focusing on his handiwork while he kept talking. "Don't worry. We're staying out of everybody's way. We even answered a few of the arson investigator's questions. We were hanging out on the other side of the lake when all the fire trucks showed up. Looks like that fire came pretty close to your house."

"A couple of hills away." Technically, he was in *her* way. Amy swallowed the temper flaring inside her. Wigging out right now would only draw KCPD's attention, and she was doing her very best to remain the cooperative witness and not become a person of interest. She gently nudged the sawhorse table back toward the wall, taking care not to spill the Spackle bucket or cans of stain on it. "The house would have been in trouble if the fire had jumped the creek bed."

"No water in the creek," Richie added before

turning on the sander and drowning out any further conversation with the machine's high-pitched drone.

The deafening whine severed the last thread of Amy's polite patience. There were already too many people in the house, invading her space, wrecking any opportunity to mourn and plan the next tasks on her things-to-do-for-Jocelyn list. The police had already contacted Jocelyn's parents in Nebraska, but Amy wanted to call them personally to share her condolences. And someone needed to notify the university and insurance adjusters to take care of the research equipment and personal belongings that had been destroyed in the fire. The house was already filled with criminologists and detectives, an arson investigator, and uniformed officers, all poking through Jocelyn's things and asking questions. She didn't need Brad and Richie here, too, acting as though it was a regular ol' workday and she hadn't lost her best friend, and that the property she was trying to protect for her grandmother hadn't almost been destroyed.

Squashing the urge to call them Frick and Frack out loud, Amy dredged up one more smile for her part-time employees. "Hey, guys. I appreciate your work ethic—" she thumbed over her shoulder to the front door "—but I need you to call it a night. We've had a rough day here. Hopefully, everyone will clear out soon, and Gran and I can have a quiet evening."

"Is Mrs. Hall here yet?" Brad asked, scanning the foyer from the front door to the rooms off the back hallway—as if her grandmother's presence could persuade him in a way Amy's request could not. He attacked the next hole with the Spackle, refusing to take the hint.

"No. But she called, and she's on her way." Not that it was any of Brad's business, but she added, "Friends are driving her home. I really need you both gone before she gets here."

"S-s-sorry about Miss Jocelyn." Richie stuttered an apology. "She was a nice lady."

"That she was," Amy agreed, raising her voice to be heard over the sander.

"She baked me cupcakes," Richie continued. "They weren't v-very good."

Despite Richie's effort to be sympathetic, Brad huffed a curse under his breath at being dismissed. His dark eyes narrowed when they came back to her. "I said it was no trouble to be here. We were just getting started. The clock's tickin' on your deadline. How the hell do you expect us to get all this woodwork and the exterior siding stained and painted by the end of the month?"

Amy bristled at the accusation in his tone. "Go ahead and log the time you were here this evening. But I need you to leave."

A thump from the ceiling above them made

Amy wonder if the detectives and CSIs had flipped the mattress off Jocelyn's bed or were moving furniture now. With the whine of the sander, the drone of voices on every floor of the house and the footsteps of all these strangers, Amy wanted to run from the chaos and lose herself in the vast solitude of the scorched wilderness or hide away in the privacy of her art studio.

But she needed to stay. For her gran. For Jocelyn. For the truth.

The sander whined like an assault against her eardrums. "Richie!"

He instantly turned the sander off, his smile sheepish as he faced her. "Yes, Miss Amy?"

Hugging her arms around her waist, she wondered at the sudden chill she felt. She hated not being in control of her environment, not having all the answers she needed. She hated that she had secrets that any one of these people might uncover if she couldn't get a grip on her panicked thoughts and emotions. "Just go," she pleaded. These two men worked for her. They weren't authorities she needed to obey, and she refused to be bullied by any man.

"We'll be back tomorrow." At last, she'd gotten through to Brad, even if he didn't seem particularly happy about being sent home. "Bright and early if O'Brien doesn't have any work for us."

"We'll be back tomorrow," Richie echoed. With a nod from Brad to put away the tools they'd gotten out, Amy wondered, not for the first time, if Richie had a diminished IQ, or if he was just a really, really shy guy with a stutter who got even more tongue-tied around women.

She couldn't fault him on his flawless work, though. The parts of the interior and exterior that had been touched were transforming the house into a beautiful, classic showplace. But despite Dale O'Brien's determination to tear it and all the outbuildings down, she needed time to recover from today's tragedy.

"Call first. You have my number, right?"

"I do," Brad conceded. "If that's what you want."

"It is. Thanks for understanding."

"Yes, ma'am. Whatever you say," Brad answered, putting on his own paint-stained ball cap and cursing under his breath. "Pack it up, Richie. We ain't wanted here, either."

"It'll only be a couple of days," Amy insisted.

"A couple of days without work means there's a bill I won't be able to pay," Brad groused. "But you do what you need to do."

Thanks for your compassion, Mr. Frick.

Amy's frayed patience took a turn into *Get the hell out of my house* territory. She bit down on the inside of her lip to keep the angry words roiling inside her from spilling out. She knew the two men weren't licensed like most of Dale O'Brien's other workers, and often took odd jobs to make ends meet. When they'd come to the house and offered their services three months ago, she'd been happy to hire them. No way was she finishing everything that needed to be done on the house by herself. Their work was solid, and their rate affordable. But right now she just needed some peace and quiet so she could try to figure out who hurt Jocelyn, and then have a good cry or cussing session to vent her grief.

But she refused to freak out or bawl in front of any of these people. Revealing her true emotions to the wrong person had made her far too vulnerable in the past. And she was done being vulnerable to anyone again.

As Brad picked up a mallet to hammer the lid back onto the can of stain they had opened, Richie stood up from the tarp he'd been folding. His cheeks glowed red in the waning daylight streaming through the windows on either side of the front door. And even though his gaze didn't linger on hers, he touched the brim of his cap and murmured, "S-sorry for your loss, Miss Amy."

Amy rewarded the compassion his partner had lacked with a smile. "Thank you, Richie."

Officer Marquette touched Amy's elbow. "Laundry room? Unless you want me to escort these two gentlemen out?"

"They'll be fine." She reached out to squeeze Richie's arm, both an apology and a thank-you, as she scooted between the two men. "This way."

After leaving Officer Marquette in the laundry

room to sort through a basket of Jocelyn's dirty clothes, Amy headed into the kitchen for a bottle of cool water. But while the cops had staked out the upstairs, members of the KCFD and Platte County Volunteer Fire Department had gathered in the kitchen to discuss their preliminary findings and pore over a map on the kitchen table.

Her gaze zeroed in on the stormy color of Mark Taylor's gray-blue eyes. Although they widened for a moment in recognition, then crinkled with a smile when he spotted her in the kitchen doorway, Fire Man Taylor looked away almost as quickly as she did. While he focused in on the conversation among the other men and woman in the room, Amy went to the refrigerator to retrieve the bottle of water she craved.

Although they now all wore black uniforms or T-shirts and utility pants instead of their firefighting gear like before, she recognized Mark, the slender blonde woman and the tank-sized man standing behind her as the firefighters who'd been on the scene to protect Dale O'Brien's subdivision when she'd driven in earlier. Mark pointed to something on a map spread across the kitchen table, and a flurry of questions and comments ensued. All of them seemed to be answering to a tall man with dark, nearly black hair with distinguished gray sideburns. Although she was curious to hear the details of the fire, possibly specifics about the one that had torched Jocelyn's car and storage shed, hearing several disturbing phrases like *no accident* and *incendiary liquids on the premises* and *where the body was found* made Amy opt for a quick escape, instead.

"Red, wait," Mark called out.

"Is that her?" another man asked.

"Amy." A strong, gentle hand wrapped around her elbow, stopping her in the door frame. She shivered at the unexpected touch of Mark Taylor's hand on her arm, feeling as though she'd spilled the cold water down the front of her. "Easy, Red. You okay?"

Red, huh? So they were doing nicknames now. She supposed that one fit. Amy wasn't sure if she'd jumped because she hadn't realized Mark had been addressing her, or if she'd suddenly realized that the attention of every firefighter in the room had shifted to her. She glanced up at the concern lining his eyes, forcing a smile. "I'm holding my own, Fire Man."

Was it a trick of her imagination, or was the only warm spot on her body her left elbow, where Mark still held her?

"Mark?" The deep voice of the man who seemed to be in charge prompted Mark to pull her around to face the other men and woman in the kitchen.

"This is Amy Hall. She was with me when we found the body."

"And you're certain that was the ignition point

of the fire?" the commander, or whatever his rank might be, asked.

"That was my observation. Although, we might need a chemical analysis to prove it. It could simply be a hot spot that was created in an effort to…" Mark released his loose grip on her arm and slipped his hand to the small of her back, where he rubbed a slow, easy circle. Nope. Not her imagination. Now her arm was as chilled as the rest of her. The elusive heat had followed the contact with Mark's hand. Amy couldn't help but tilt her chin to the firefighter at her side as his voice trailed away. She found his gaze locked on to hers, the grim set of his expression apologetic. "In an effort to hide the body." His big shoulders lifted with a shrug. "Sorry, Red."

Amy stepped away to concentrate on opening her water as her mind filled with the image of a charred skeleton and the soot-stained steel necklace she'd held in her hand. But her hands were shaking too badly to twist the lid off. When Mark plucked the bottle from her grasp and opened it for her, all she could do was nod her thanks.

"Miss Hall?" The man whom the others had been deferring to spoke directly to her, asking for her attention. "I'm sorry about your friend. My name is Gideon Taylor." Another Taylor? Wow. Small world. "When the police are finished with you, I'd like to ask you a few questions, as well. If you're up to it," he added kindly. Although, she got the distinct impression he expected her to say yes.

They didn't think she or her grandmother had anything to do with Jocelyn's death, did they? But she wanted answers as much as anyone else in this house did. Maybe more. She drank a swallow of the cold water before answering. "Of course." She glanced over at Mark, who still seemed to be apologizing for something she hadn't quite grasped yet. "I'll be outside when you're finished here. I could use some fresh air."

"I'll find you," Mark answered. His tone seemed to promise something more than simply fetching her for the next interrogation when the arson investigator was ready.

With a nod, Amy headed out to the front porch, holding the door for Brad and Richie as they carried their toolboxes down the front steps to Brad's beat-up car. Brad grumbled an order to *kick it into gear* and the other shot her a curious look. Amy followed them to the edge of the porch as the grumbling grew into a full-fledged argument about *stupid luck* and *no respect* and women not knowing their own mind. With that last insulting comment, Richie shushed Brad. "Miss Lissette helped us out today. Don't forget that."

"Yeah, but you've got to push them to do what they're supposed to," Brad groused.

"I think she's nice," Richie argued, defending whoever Lissette might be. "So's Miss Amy. You're bein' mean. And she can hear you."

Both men looked back at her from the open trunk of the car, and Amy held their gaze.

"Yeah, I heard you," she whispered under her breath.

Although she doubted her voice had carried as far as theirs, her attitude was crystal clear. Brad waved Richie into the car and slammed the trunk shut. Then he climbed behind the wheel and drove away in a plume of dust, turning onto the crumbling asphalt road at the bottom of the hill.

When the dust cleared, Amy discovered that she still wasn't alone. Beyond the burned-out shell and dilapidated remains of the old lake rental properties her grandfather had once managed, beyond the lake itself, she spotted another vehicle—a dust-coated white pickup with the O'Brien Construction logo painted on the side—parked near the office trailer at the edge of the Copper Lake subdivision.

Although the distance was too great to read any expression, she recognized the boxy form of Dale O'Brien lounging against the bed of the truck. He was talking on his cell phone, but she knew he was watching her because he touched his fingers to the brim of his white construction helmet and saluted her. Still on his phone after that little greeting, he straightened and circled around to climb in behind the steering wheel. Why was he still here? Was there any significance to him waiting to make contact with her before clearing out? Who exactly was he talking to, and did it have anything to do with her or Jocelyn or the fire?

She'd like to think he was chatting with an insurance adjuster, but she knew damn well the man had spies. Maybe he was doing his own dirty work, tracking every movement to and from the house, ready to report the slightest legal infraction, the slightest encroachment across a property line that might put him one step closer to purchasing the land all the way around the lake. He started the engine, but remained in the truck, finally focusing on his call and not on her.

Inhaling her first deep breath in hours, Amy turned her face to the fading warmth of the sun, watching the glowing ball shimmer and change colors as it sank below the horizon. Usually the pinks and oranges and hints of deep turquoise as the sky darkened inspired her with images of the art she loved to create. But tonight, the sunset simply marked the end of a very long, very traumatic day.

She heard the crunch of footsteps on the front sidewalk. "Now what have you done?"

Amy groaned at the gravelly voice accosting her from the bottom of the porch steps. So much for solitude. "Mr. Sanders. Is there something I could help you with?"

The lanky, slightly stooped older black man who rented one of their remaining bungalows down by the lake glared at her from beneath two white eyebrows that reminded her of fuzzy albino caterpillars. "I just got back to my house. There's no water pressure there."

Seriously? He wanted her to play landlord and come fix something right now? "Mr. Sanders, KCFD and the Platte County volunteers have been fighting wildfires all day. I'm guessing it will take time for the pressure in the pipes to build up again. I'll look at it in the morning if you're still having issues. You can come into the house and use one of the bathrooms here if you need to."

He grunted a noise that sounded like she'd given him the unsatisfactory answer he'd expected. A widower who'd worked half his life in a manufacturing plant in the city, he'd answered her ad for an affordable rental back when her strategy had been to fill the empty homes on the north side of the lake to dissuade Dale O'Brien from expanding his subdivision. When Mr. Sanders signed the leasing agreement, Amy thought she'd met a new friend who appreciated the quiet and emptiness of the countryside beyond the suburbs and downtown KC area. But Gerald Sanders took his loner status to the extreme, making her wonder what had happened in his life to make him such a cranky recluse. If it wasn't for complaints like this, she never saw her closest neighbor at all. He even stuck his rent check in the mailbox when she wasn't at home.

When he buried his hands in the deep pockets of his overalls, making no effort to leave, Amy studied him a little more closely. "Was there something else?"

He worked those bushy brows in and out of a frown before he asked, "Is your grandmother all right?" Was he worried about her? When had he become friends with her gran? Had the two seventy-somethings ever exchanged more than a few words?

Still, his concern was the most humane thing she'd heard him say. "Yes. She's been at a friend's all day."

"Good. When I saw all these official vehicles, I worried something might have happened to Comfort."

"I'll let her know you asked about her. She'll appreciate that."

"Like it isn't bad enough I have construction noise and your hammering coming into my house all day long. Now I've got the police and Kansas City firefighters knocking on my door, asking if I've seen anything suspicious." And poof! Just like that, the human connection she'd felt for a few moments vanished. "I rented that house out here to be alone, to get away from interruptions like that." He leaned in slightly, somehow giving the impression he was looking down his nose at her, even though she stood on the steps above him. "You want me to tell them just who I've seen wandering around the premises at night?"

Amy's hand fisted around her water bottle, crumpling the plastic in her fist. "I live here. If I want to go for a walk at midnight or work late in my studio, that's my right. And it's *my* business. I don't need you spying on me."

"Don't you go gettin' growly with me, girl. You know I'm the only tenant who's stuck by your gran after the stables and the old foreman's house burned down. You need my income. That means you need to show me a little respect. That means you keep the cops away from me. Unless Comfort needs something, I want you and all these people to leave me alone."

"You're not the only one who's being asked a lot of questions, Mr. Sanders. Why don't you go home and lock your door and be your old grouchy self without bothering me."

"Young lady—"

"I'm sorry. I'm grieving for a friend and ticked off that anyone would want to hurt her. I can't handle your accusations right now." Amy stormed down the steps and hurried past him, needing to get away from all the chaos before her head exploded.

I'll find you.

Mark Taylor's words echoed in her head as she ran. She didn't care that he'd have to chase her down again, that she wouldn't be where she'd promised to wait.

If she felt eyes on her, she convinced herself it was Gerald Sanders, or Dale O'Brien, watching her as he chatted in his truck. Or maybe Brad and Richie had circled back to plead for a paying job. Maybe Derek hadn't returned to the city after all. Maybe he was parked on some dusty side road or behind a hill, wanting to be close to the woman he'd loved and the mystery of her death. Or maybe it was the cops upstairs, or the firefighters downstairs, or…

"Damn it." Amy jogged around to the buildings behind the house, fighting the instinct that said something sinister, something much more malevolent than a bossy firefighter with an interesting face and a hot body, was keeping her in his sights.

Chapter Five

Amy stood at the vise on the workbench in her converted art studio, losing herself in the tangy scent of burning metal and the hiss and pop of gas from her oxyacetylene torch as she heated a sheet of copper to create a muted rainbow of red, pink and turquoise on the body of her latest sculpture.

She'd opened the window above her workbench to let the fumes dissipate into the still night air outside. Even though the sun had sunk below the horizon, she hadn't turned on anything more than the work light that hung from a nearby shelf, relying on the bright beam of light from her welding torch to illuminate her work. Night and shadows had settled around her like a cloak, and she relished the isolating feeling.

It wasn't comfort she needed so much as time to think. She needed time without strangers taking over her grandmother's house or familiar faces like Brad Frick and Mr. Sanders choosing this night to push her for things that were scarcely a priority for her right now.

Right now, she needed to remember. As she virtually painted the strokes of color by heating different parts of the metal to varying temperatures, she recalled her time here this morning, sketching out the whimsical piece, selecting the copper and anchoring it into place. But before she had been able to turn on her equipment and begin the actual piece, the call to evacuate the premises had come. That was when she'd made her first call to Jocelyn, warning her to get out of the wildfire's path. That was the last time she'd spoken to her friend.

That last chat with Jocelyn felt like a lifetime ago. What a hell of a long day.

Tears pooled in the bottom of the safety goggles she wore beneath her welding helmet. They tickled her cheeks as she thought of all the conversations they'd shared that had been about nothing. Now, knowing she'd never see another text about some gross bug Jocelyn had stumbled upon in the old apple orchard, or never hear another excited voice mail about a botanical or geologic theorem she'd proved that Amy didn't understand, Amy wished she'd paid closer attention—that she'd understood the importance of every message.

She shoved her gloved fingers up beneath the face shield of her helmet to swipe at the tears blurring her vision. Damn it. Hadn't she already cried enough today? Crying was more sensitive Jocelyn's thing—not wild-child Amy. They'd always been opposites. The science geek and the eccentric artist. A quiet brunette and a mouthy redhead. She and Jocelyn couldn't have been more different. And yet they couldn't have been any closer. Who would ever want to hurt her friend? Jocelyn had never been in trouble with the cops. She'd never had a run-in with her professors or been in a relationship that had gone sideways. She'd never had an unkind word for anybody.

Amy was the one who spoke her mind and fought for lost causes and made enemies.

But Jocelyn was the one who'd had her head bashed in and had been set on fire.

It simply wasn't fair. Amy pulled the torch away from the metal when she let the hissing line of flame overheat one spot to a deep blood red. She cursed behind her mask. "Nothing symbolic about that, huh? Did you see something you shouldn't have, Joss? Was there some secret you never told me? Is there a monster out there who set his sights on you? Did you know? Were you surprised? Did you suffer?"

More tears, full of anger rather than grief, steamed up her goggles.

Amy drew the flame across the copper again, determined to find solace in her work if she couldn't find answers. She had almost blinked her vision clear when the door behind her swung open and the overhead light came on. "Damn it, Mr. Sanders! Have you ever heard of knocking?" She spun around, her temper flaring. "I said I'd get to it in the morn—"

Not a bushy-eyebrowed geezer who'd gotten on her last nerve.

Her visitor was a tall, broad-shouldered firefighter with short, spiky dark hair that needed to see a comb. Or her fingers.

Amy blinked and immediately twisted the valve to shut off the gas flow to her torch and kill the flame. She eyed the bulky gloves that protected her hands and effectively kept her from touching anything. Yet she could feel the tingling in her fingertips, as though she had brushed them through the wiry disarray on top of Mark Taylor's head. Where had that impulse come from? Why was she having any impulses at all concerning the Captain Good Guy Bossy Buttinsky filling the doorway?

"Hey, Red. I thought you'd disappeared on me."

"Fire Man," she acknowledged, pushing up the face mask and removing her helmet. She set it on the workbench before removing her goggles and hanging them on the pegboard above the bench.

"Fire Woman. Didn't know you were a welder. I followed the smell of the gas and flames, and I wanted to make sure you were okay."

She stowed the torch on its metal hook and

turned back to her workbench to unwind the vise and pick up the sheet of copper. She carried it over to the concrete blocks near the old garage door to cool. "Didn't know you were keeping tabs on me. I'll be sure to file a travel report the next time I go into my own backyard."

The door closed behind him. "I did knock. You probably couldn't hear me over the equipment. I take it this Mr. Sanders is a troublemaker? Need me to go beat him up for you?"

She wondered how Mark Taylor could make his deep, steady voice sound so comforting, even with the teasing and probing questions.

Amy shook her head, fighting the urge to smile. "It would hardly be a fair fight. He's closer to eighty than he is seventy. And you're what…? Thirty?"

"Twenty-eight," he answered. "I bet I could still take him."

A small laugh bubbled up, catching on the grief and anger constricting her throat and coming out in an embarrassing hiccup. "I bet you could." She pulled off the insulated gloves she wore and tossed them onto the workbench before pushing a stray tendril of her own hair off her face. "I'd say come in, but since you're already here, I'll just offer you a seat." She pointed to the stool at her drafting table and the denim couch decorated with colorful pillows along the wall opposite the workbench. "Your choices are limited, but comfortable."

He studied her face, no doubt taking in her red-rimmed eyes and the tear tracks crystallizing on her cheeks. "Old Man Sanders made you cry?"

Amy quickly ducked her face away from his curious gaze and busied herself unzipping the faded and stained blue coveralls her grandfather had once worn. She stripped down to the shorts and tank top she wore underneath before putting away her torch, mask and gloves, ensuring the gas canister was shut down correctly and her gear was neatly stowed. "Gerald Sanders is our tenant. He lives in the white house down by the lake. He chose tonight to complain about the plumbing. I couldn't deal with him right now, so I came here to work."

"Someone actually lives in one of those places?"

She splashed some cool water from the slop sink on her face before realizing she hadn't set a clean towel out. Instead of digging through the refinished dresser that sat in the corner, she grabbed the blouse she'd worn earlier to dab her skin dry. "We used to have three more tenants until the foreman's house burned down. A single man who worked on a neighboring farm and two other guys who work on a highway construction crew. We're cheaper than a hotel for a long-term stay." She pulled the damp blouse on over her tank top and turned to face him. "They're nicer on the inside than they are the outside. And being so close to the lake has always been a draw."

"It is a pretty lake. The fishing any good there?"

"It's mostly crappie. Better for fun than eating. Grandpa tried to get catfish going in the lake, but no one's caught one that I know of. Of course, with the water levels down, nobody's fished there at all this summer."

He moved to her workbench, inspecting her tools and the cubbies and crates where she stored a variety of scrap metals and found objects. "Do you fish?"

"I used to when Grandpa was alive. I loved going out on the water with him." She tied the tails of the blouse around her waist and picked up the bottle of water she'd taken from the kitchen to down the last of it. She hadn't known how ugly the world could be when Grandpa Leland was still alive. Now he was gone, and her life had changed drastically from the dreamy-eyed tomboy's he'd raised. "Those were simpler times. Are you a fisherman?"

She looked up in time to see a shadow pass across his face. Before she could act on the curious compassion that squeezed her raw heart, Mark straightened to his full height and reached into his back pocket.

"Sorry if I hit a nerve. Mark—?"

"Here." He pushed a black bandanna into her hand. He pointed to his own cheek, indicating the droplets of water or tears that glistened on her face. "My grandmother said I should always carry a handkerchief in case somebody needed to wipe their eyes or blow their nose or, you know, apply a tourniquet. Frankly, I use a tissue for all that. Not the tourniquet, of course. Never holds." Amy almost smiled at the silly remark, even though she understood the diversion for what it was—an attempt to deflect her concern. "I'm glad I have one with me today."

"You're trying to rescue me again." She dabbed the soft cotton against her feverish eyes and nose, relishing its soothing comfort. "I swear I haven't cried this much since Grandpa died. I'm used to being stronger than this. But thanks."

"What made the foreman's house burn? Faulty wiring? Someone falling asleep with a cigarette?"

The flare of sympathy she'd felt died with the reminder that opening her heart to someone only set her up to be hurt or taken advantage of again. Why would he ask that? Was he really here to check on her welfare? Or was this part of the KCFD investigation?

Did he really want to mention the word *arson*? The source of that fire had been confirmed, though who had set the blaze was yet to be determined.

Amy tilted her face to study him. Same KCFD

T-shirt. Same broad shoulders. Same short crop of spiky brown hair. This time she noticed the interesting bump on the bridge of his nose that indicated a fight or accident in years past. And the stubble of a five o'clock beard shadowed his jaw, making the crooked grin that softened his firm mouth stand out against his taut skin. Damn her traitorous hormones for being attracted to Mark Taylor. If this man was using subterfuge to get some answers, he was awfully good at hiding it. And what secret had he shuttered away when they'd been talking about something as inane as fishing? "What are you really doing here, Fire Man? Is this part of my interview? If so, I don't know anything about the fire at the old foreman's house. Only that the two highway workers renting the place were gone that weekend, so no one was hurt."

"I'm just checking on you, if that's okay," he answered, instead of pushing for details she couldn't give and suspicions she wouldn't share. "I grew up in a family of cops and firefighters. I know days like this can be pretty intense." He looked around, taking in the rest of her supplies. He studied the works in progress, the hodgepodge of furniture, and the chains and pulley system suspended from the ceiling left over from when this workshop had been Grandpa Leland's. "What is this place? A machine shop? One of those she-sheds?"

"It used to be the garage where my grandfather worked on his tractor and other small equipment. Now it's my art studio. It has good light when I open the windows and garage entrance, doors I can lock." Which, apparently, she should have done if she'd really wanted to be alone.

"That explains the new roof and why this place has been better taken care of than the other outbuildings."

Steeling herself against the probing questions he sneaked into their casual conversation, Amy downed a sip of water and sat on one end of the couch. "Why is KCFD still here? The wildfire is out, isn't it?"

He folded his long, sturdy body down on the cushion beside her. "This isn't about wildfires and drought conditions anymore."

No. It was about murder and arson. "Tell me about it. The cops are asking lots of questions, going through everything in Jocelyn's room. I don't know what they think they'll find. She kept scientific journals, not a diary."

"Did she have a boyfriend? Maybe they're looking for a connection there?"

"So, this *is* an interview."

"I'm just making conversation."

"Does that all-American good-guy charm work for you with other women? Get them to drop their guard so they'll answer all your questions?"

He gave her an exaggerated wink. "You think I'm charming?"

It was such a nerdy maneuver that Amy laughed before she could stop herself. He surprised her by touching the tip of his finger to the point of her chin and mirroring her smile. "That's better."

For several endless moments, Amy stared into gray-blue eyes and wondered at the sudden infusion of heat that seemed to be drawn through her blood to the simple press of a gentle, calloused finger against her skin. But then she blinked, and her thoughts suddenly filled with images of the last man she'd foolishly found so captivating.

Amy pushed to her feet, carried her empty water bottle over to the bin beside the trash and crushed it in her hands before tossing it inside. Mark Taylor and Preston Worth weren't anything alike. Not in age. Not in looks. Certainly not in personality.

Preston's prematurely gray hair and striking features matched his vast knowledge of art and his travels around the world. He was sophisticated and charismatic. He'd taken Amy under his wing, encouraging both her talent and her eagerness to learn. He'd flattered her pale skin and Rubenesque figure, demanding she sit for him while he painted her. She'd felt beautiful in the studio and in the bedroom under his tutelage. She'd blossomed in his bright, colorful world.

And then one day she woke up.

Amy flashed back to her last scary encounter with the professor she'd fallen in love with. She'd never expected Preston to get violent when she broke off the affair after discovering she wasn't the only muse he'd taken to bed. She might still be in grad school, working on her PhD, if Professor Worth hadn't threatened to fail her on her art thesis and studio show. Hell, she might still be painting on a canvas instead of on her grandmother's house. Fortunately, she'd found a new medium she loved with her welded sculptures and jewelry making. There was strength in fire and metal, a strength she'd needed to get through the hell of taking down a powerful man and seeing her lifelong dreams go up in flames.

Because Preston Worth had taken far more from her than her doctorate and her watercolors. He'd taken her hopeful innocence about the world. He'd stolen her ability to trust and her willingness to give her heart to another man. She'd burned the remnants of that life down to the ground, but she couldn't purge the feelings of self-doubt and mistrust that lingered in the aftermath.

She'd reported the assault and subsequent threats meant to keep her quiet about it. She'd gotten him fired from Williams University, in fact. Amy had even gone through the preliminary stages of his criminal trial. But then Grandpa had passed, and Gran needed her, and… Preston Worth scared her in a way that most men did not. Although the charges against him had been negotiated down to lesser charges—a year in prison and probation—and he'd gone through a mandated anger management class, with Preston's temper, she could see him committing a crime of passion like she'd seen today. But Jocelyn didn't have anyone like that in her life. At least no one Amy was aware of…unless Derek Roland's personality had changed 180 degrees.

"Amy?" She startled at the brush of Mark's fingers on her shoulders. He held his hands up in apology when she spun around. "Sorry. Where'd you go?"

She wasn't about to share her trip down nightmare lane with a man she'd only known for a day, a man who was weaving a spell of attraction and security around her she couldn't afford to get too comfortable with. "I was thinking about who'd want to hurt Jocelyn and was coming up with zilch."

It wasn't too far from the truth. Mark Taylor didn't need to know that few people would have been surprised if she'd turned up as the victim today.

His gray-blue eyes narrowed as if he knew she wasn't telling the complete truth. "Are you sure you're all right? Your skin's a little pale. No af-

tereffects from today? I've got paramedic training. I can get my kit."

"No. I don't need first aid." Amy waved her
hands, urging him out of her personal space and
dismissing his concern. She folded the black bandanna into a neat square, then unfolded it again
and tied it around her wrist when he refused her
offer to return it. "Why are you here, Fire Man?
Babysitting me? Making sure I don't run off before the chief interviews me?" If he was staying
put, then she would move away. She made a show
of fluffing the decorative pillows on the sofa.
"Are you an arson investigator, too?"

He shook his head. "I was the first firefighter
on the scene at the shed. They needed my report.
I told them what we moved to get to the body, and
so on. Besides, I rode up here with my brother
and he's still inside, keeping an eye on Mom."

"Your mom and dad and brother are firefighters, too?"

"Yeah." He crossed to inspect the valves on
the oxyacetylene and Argon-CO2 canisters she
used for different welding jobs. She knew she'd
stored all her equipment according to regula-
tion, but still, it made her feel a little less like
she was under official scrutiny when he nodded
and moved on to study her sketches on the drafting table. "My dad's the chief arson investigator.
You spoke to him in the kitchen."

Amy hugged a turquoise batik pillow to her

chest. "That sexy guy with the silver sideburns is your dad?"

"Um, I don't really think of him in those terms. But man of few words? Large and in charge?" She nodded at the apt description. "Yep. Gideon Taylor is my dad."

"You don't look like him." Except for the sexy part. She should be more worried about how her brain kept focusing on liking this guy instead of maintaining her defenses. Sure, Mark Taylor gave her interesting ideas for a piece she wanted to sculpt. His face reflected the cool tones of the overhead light and created mysterious shadows in the hollows beneath his cheekbones and jaw. Maybe she'd take up painting again, to see if she could capture the beautiful stormy-sky color of his eyes. Suddenly aware of just how thoroughly she was studying him, she set the pillow down. "And the blonde who was bossing all the fire-fighters around earlier is your mom?"

"I look even less like her." He reappeared beside her, holding a pencil sketch from her drafting table. "This is like the pendant you wear around your neck. Your friend had one, too. You made them?"

Amy nodded, her fingers automatically going to the matching knot of steel resting against her cleavage. "I work mostly in metals now. Everything from big sculptures to intricate jewelry."

"You know the crime lab will still have to do

an autopsy on the remains. Identifying her by the necklace alone won't hold up in court. But it does give the ME a lead on whose dental records to pull."

She felt light-headed at the thought of the medical examiner doing further damage to the body she'd found. "I suspected as much. But it's her. I know it is."

"Your drawings are good," Mark pointed out after several moments of silence, no doubt wanting to divert her thoughts from the images an autopsy conjured. "So, art is what you do for a living?"

"I make decent money at it. Not enough to pay for all the home repairs I've taken on. But I could live on it if I had to." She didn't want to talk about herself anymore. She didn't want to talk about his father's investigation, either. She carried the drawing back to the table. "Who's the guy who looked like he had to duck and turn sideways to get through the door?"

"My brother Matt." He saw her frowning at the idea of him and Matt coming from the petite blonde. "We're adopted. Matt and I are blood brothers, too. Our parents died in a fire when we were little. I barely remember them. Alex and Pike are part of the Taylor tribe, too. They're cops with KCPD. All four of us were adopted from the same foster home where Mom grew up."

Adopted? Foster care? Amy slowly revised her

all-American-hero impression of Mark Taylor. Not only was his face incredibly interesting, but there seemed to be some interesting dimensions to his history and personality, as well. A fascinating subject with complex layers beneath his good-guy facade—and those impressive arms and shoulders? She wondered if he was hairy-chested, waxed clean or something in between. Any way she imagined it, he really would make an attractive model to pose for her art.

"Would you like to take a shower?" Mark asked.

Amy gasped at the unexpected question. She smoothed her hair behind her ears and shook her tangled ponytail loose behind her back, wondering if she'd heard him correctly. She'd just been thinking about how physical he was and how she'd like to strip him down to sketch and sculpt him.

But then she felt the sticky grit of soot and dusty earth clinging to her hair and realized she was a mess. "Why?" She tugged the collar of her soiled blouse up to her nose. "Do I smell?"

He laughed. "Only like anybody else who's been dealing with a fire. Seriously, you're lucky you're not downwind of me." He held his hands up in mock surrender, taking any sting from his words. "Back in the kitchen, I could tell you needed a few minutes away from all the drama. Just now you said you needed some time alone. I can clear the house if you want me to."

She arched a doubting eyebrow. "You're not the man in charge."

"No, but I'm in pretty good with the guy who is. I'd ask everyone to give you some space and stand watch outside your bathroom door. Promise I wouldn't peek." His rugged cheeks softened with the barest hint of pink. A man who blushed? Could Captain Good Guy here speak any more clearly to her artistic impulses?

"You are determined to save me, aren't you?"

"My mom does that. Bubble baths are her thing. Growing up, none of us even dared knock on the door when she was in her sanctuary. And believe me, as much as she loves us, she needed a break from the four of us boys and Dad every now and then."

Amy's meager defenses against this man were crumbling. "You're giving away state secrets, Fire Man. I know all about your family now."

He perched on the edge of the sofa, inviting her to sit beside him again. "Then tell me something about you besides working with power tools and making art. I'm the baby. Of my generation, at any rate." Oh, there was nothing babyish about him. "You got any siblings to pick on you?"

Why was this man so easy to talk to? If the police or arson investigator wanted answers from her, they'd be smart to send in Mark. Even though every survival instinct inside her warned her not to give in to his goofy charm and apparent kindness, she shook her head. "Only child. My parents died when I was little, too. A car accident. Gran and Grandpa raised me. Grandpa passed away two years ago."

That shadow of pain shuddered across his face again before his crooked mouth widened with a grin that couldn't quite erase the pain she'd glimpsed. "Family is everything, isn't it? Me? I've got uncles and aunts and siblings coming out my ears. But I wouldn't trade the madness of a Sunday family dinner or Labor Day reunion for the world." He shrugged. "Of course, I'm not sure exactly how that's going to play out now that my grandma is moving to a new home. It won't be the same."

"It's the people, not the place or the activity, that matter." A lesson her grandparents had taught her as a child.

"Yep. Still, when one of those people is missing…"

Amy nodded. "Jocelyn was the closest thing to a sister I'll ever have. Now Gran's all I have left."

"You live here with your grandmother?"

"I moved back when I left grad school at Williams University, after my grandfather passed. Mutual benefits. This way, I don't worry about her being out here by herself."

"And she had the perfect location for your art studio."

"Exactly." Amy fiddled with her pendant again,

wishing she could rebuild her own heart the way she'd crafted the coiled tendrils around the abstract chunk of steel. "We're all each other has."

"I lost my grandfather a couple of months ago." The way he worked the tight line of his jaw made her think he was still in the throes of grief. "He was one of the greatest men I ever knew."

She reached over to squeeze his thigh. Exhaustion must be making her a fool to care about his pain. Or maybe it was simple empathy because of the loss she'd suffered today. "I'm sorry."

He placed his hand over hers. It was a workingman's hand, yet it was as finely shaped as the rest of his body. "Thanks."

When he flipped his palm to link their fingers together, she didn't pull away. Despite the instincts that screamed at her to guard her emotions, getting close to Mark Taylor felt so natural, so right. She felt his sadness as clearly as her own. "Are you okay?"

"Hey, I'm here to cheer you up," he teased.

Amy didn't laugh. "I told you I don't need to be rescued."

"Give me a break. It's what I do." He tightened his grip around hers briefly before pulling away and checking his watch. "I hate to do this to you, but, if you're ready, I do need you to go talk to Dad."

She stood when he did. "Might as well get it

over with. I don't know what I can tell him that I didn't already tell the police."

"Just be honest. And if you don't have an answer, it's okay to say that, too." Mark helped her close the windows. After locking up her studio, they crossed down to the long gravel driveway and headed back to the house.

"I'm glad you were there when I found Jocelyn," she admitted as he fell into step beside her. "But, for the record, I would have gotten past the shock. I would have called the police and made my way back here without your help."

He grinned at her over the jut of his shoulder. "Message received. You're a tough chick and I'm a Neanderthal."

"Don't put words in my mouth. It's not an insult. I just meant that I can do the rescuing and cheering up, too."

"It's okay to let someone help you when you need it, Amy. Family has taught me that."

Then why hadn't his family helped him with the grief or guilt or whatever emotion had shadowed his face earlier?

Amy grasped his hand and stopped, silently asking him to face her. When he did, she gave in to the urge that had taunted her all evening and reached up to smooth the messy spikes of hair that stood up above his forehead. She hadn't expected a simple neatening up could feel so intimate. She hadn't expected him to reach out and capture a loose lock of her hair between his fingers and inspect its color and texture before tucking it behind her ear, either.

He was taking care of her. Rescuing her. Seducing her without even trying.

"Look, Fire Man—Mark…" She grabbed his errant hand and squeezed it between both of hers, stilling his caress, whether it had been intended or accidental. She tilted her chin the short distance necessary to meet his curious gaze. "I need you to stop being such a good guy. Nothing's going to happen between us. Nothing should. You don't want to get involved with me. I can be a lot of trouble."

"Who told you that?"

"Seriously. I don't think I'm your type, and…"

"And what?" He switched grips so that he was holding her fingers in his. This would be so much easier if she could boss him around. He was patient, yes, had a cheesy sense of humor, but he clearly wasn't a pushover. And that was part of the problem. "Are you thinking you like me, too?"

"Too?" Her eyes widened at the implication. He was feeling this foolish connection just like she was. "This has been an extremely unusual day. We were thrown together by awful circumstances. You made me laugh, you annoyed the hell out of me, you comforted me—and I'm grateful. If I leaned on you a little bit, or there's some heat-of-the-moment, opposites-attracting kind of thing going on, I blame it on the day." She wished the breeze hadn't kicked up just then, blowing the dust that billowed up from an approaching car in the driveway over them, and kicking up those coffee-colored spikes of hair her fingers itched to smooth into place again. She pulled away, wisely breaking all contact with him. "I'm not looking for a relationship. I've taken advantage of your kindness more than once today. I don't want you to think I'm leading you on."

"Fair enough," he agreed. He nodded toward her art studio. "But I wasn't the only one doling out comfort back there. Don't I get a say in this heat-of-the-moment, opposites-attracting thing, too?"

Amy was saved from coming up with another reasonable argument that would shut down this budding attraction by the sound of her grandmother's voice. "Amy?"

At the honk of a car horn, Amy turned and waved a thanks to the friends who had dropped Comfort Hall off and were now driving away. Leaving Mark behind, she hurried to meet the slender, slightly stooped woman with the circular lime green eyeglasses, a mannish snow-white haircut and cropped linen pants that gave her grandmother a distinctly boho vibe.

"Gran." Amy wound her arms around Comfort's slender shoulders and felt those familiar loving arms wrap around her in a tight hug. "I'm so glad you're here."

"Oh, baby, I'm so sorry. What a horrible accident." She pulled back far enough to study Amy's face and inspect the evidence of tears there. "Jocelyn was such a fine young woman."

She pulled her in for another hug, and Amy held on when she felt the shudder of grief tremble through her grandmother's body. They kissed each other's cheek before Amy pulled away to deliver the grim news. "It wasn't an accident, Gran. The police are in the preliminary stages of their investigation, but someone attacked Joss. The fire was an attempt to cover up the crime scene. I think her killer thought the police would blame it on the other fires we've been battling."

"Murder?" Comfort pressed a hand over her heart. "That poor girl. Who would want to hurt Jocelyn?" Dropping her voice to a whisper, Comfort peeked over the top of her glasses. "An arson fire? They don't suspect—"

"That's why I wanted to warn you about all the people in the house tonight." Amy cut her off before her grandmother could finish that sentence. She tilted her head toward the man waiting patiently behind her. "They're trying to figure it all out."

"I see." Comfort's hazel eyes darted past Amy to assess Mark's casual uniform before hugging her one more time. Gran understood better than anyone how much trouble Amy could be in if certain elements of her past came to light, whether she was innocent or not. "How are you holding up, dear?"

"I'm okay." She looked back to invite Mark to join them. "I made a new friend today. He tried to rescue me earlier."

The older woman snickered, not bothering to hide her amusement. "How did that go?"

"He's been…patient…with me." She gestured to make the introductions. "Gran—Comfort Hall—this is Mark Taylor. He's a KCFD firefighter."

Gran smiled broadly when Mark took her hand. "I can see that. Nice uniform."

"Mrs. Hall."

"Aren't you a tall, hunky drink of water." Her smile didn't dim as she drew back. "I'm available, you know." Oh, my gosh, was that a nudge on Amy's elbow? "So is my granddaughter."

"Gran!"

Mark grinned. "I believe you're flirtin' with me, ma'am."

"Is it working, handsome?"

His cheekbones warmed with a sweetly vulnerable blush.

Amy rushed to his defense, hoping to tone down the obvious matchmaking. "He's not handsome, Gran." When Comfort arched a fine, snowy white brow above her glasses, Amy realized that her words might not have come out the way she'd intended. Not wanting to offend Mark or endure a lecture on politeness from her grandmother, Amy hastened to explain. "His face is interesting." Ever the artist, Amy touched Mark's face to point out exactly what made his looks so compelling. "Strong angles and shading. The intriguing bump on his nose. Those gray-blue eyes. The design of his face is better than handsome." When she felt the stubble of his beard tickling her fingertips, and saw those gorgeous eyes boring into hers, Amy quickly pulled away. Now they were both blushing. She squared her back against the firefighter who was doing crazy things to her vows to swear off men and wrapped an arm around her grandmother's shoulders. "We'd better get you inside. The police and arson investigator might want to ask you some questions about Jocelyn."

"Did you make coffee for them?" Comfort asked.

"No. I was trying to stay out of the way." When Comfort stopped at the bottom of the porch steps, Amy confessed the truth. "All right. I was hiding out for a few minutes, trying to get my act together. I'm guessing someone sent Mark out to fetch me."

"I came of my own volition," Mark volunteered, unable to avoid eavesdropping. "I swear."

Comfort lowered her voice to a whisper. "He seems like a nice man."

"Doesn't matter," Amy whispered right back.

A little bit of heartbreak creased her face before Comfort squeezed Amy's hand. On a mission now, she turned and climbed the porch steps. "I'd better get a pot started for our guests. You get cleaned up and come help me."

"What is it with everyone wanting me naked in a shower?"

Her grandmother turned at the front door. "Who wants to get you naked?"

"Gran!" Amy heard the words and turned to Mark to apologize. "I mean, offering me a private bath…" Nope. That wasn't any better. "I will stop talking now."

Mark nudged a pebble with his foot, the blush on his cheeks as evident as the fire heating her own. But her grandmother was grinning from ear to ear as Amy glared daggers at her. "I don't know what you two have been talking about, but it sounds mighty intriguing. It was nice to meet you, Mark."

"Ma'am."

Comfort winked behind her glasses. "Invite your friend to stay if he wants."

When the front door closed behind her grandmother, Amy quickly apologized to Mark. "That was awkward."

Being the unfailingly good guy that he was,

Mark grinned and put her at ease. "Don't worry. I know a thing or two about grandmothers. Relentless matchmakers. Always worried you're going to wind up alone."

"Or unfed." She shrugged. "And unwashed, apparently."

His easy, deep-pitched laughter made her smile. Amy extended her hand. Nothing could ever come of this chemistry they seemed to share, but she had enjoyed *most* of her time with Mark Taylor. "Thank you, Fire Man."

"I was just doing—"

"Don't say you were just doing your job. I was losing it earlier, when I couldn't find Jocelyn. I *did* lose it when we did." The polite thing to do would be to release his hand. And yet she didn't. Instead she turned it over and traced the shape of his knuckles with her fingertips. "I'm sorry I didn't listen to you then. But I couldn't think straight. I was frantic with the need to—"

"Find your friend." His grip tightened around hers a moment before he proved the stronger of them and pulled away to prop his hands at his waist. "I'll give you a pass on that one today, too. Your reputation as a stubbornly independent woman is still intact."

"Thanks." Amy tugged on the bandanna knotted at her wrist. "And thanks for not letting me be alone with my thoughts for too long tonight."

"Why does Dale O'Brien call you Crazy Amy?"

"Because he's a jerk?" The abrupt change in topic when she kept trying to say goodbye reminded her that he could be part of his father's investigation. But O'Brien was a sore spot for her. "Because I don't bow down at his feet like he's the power broker he thinks he is? I work odd hours in my studio when I get an inspiration, so he thinks I'm spying on him and sabotaging his construction sites if I'm up in the middle of the night? He doesn't understand the words *no sale*? Take your pick. And yes, I might have given him a little aesthetic advice on the design of his blocky, modern houses so that they fit in better with the lake and wilderness surrounding us. His designs are like sticking a concrete cinder block in the middle of a Monet painting. I don't think he appreciated my input. I can be obstinate sometimes."

"Really? You? Speaking your mind?" Mark teased.

"You don't know me, Fire Man," she teased right back.

"I know you don't take orders very well."

"No. But I can be reasoned with." She frowned, remembering that he hadn't been reasonable at all when he'd first chased her down during her search for Jocelyn. "Would you really have thrown me over your shoulder and carried me away from the fire?"

"Yes."

"I'm a big girl," she argued.

"I'm a big boy," he responded without batting an eye. "Picking you up would not be a problem for me." His strong arms swelled in size as he crossed them over his chest, more than proving his point.

Something deep inside Amy's womb fluttered at the blatant show of masculinity. *Not. Your. Type.* Why couldn't she keep a coherent thought around this man? Or just walk away from him? "I don't know whether that's freakin' hot or if I should be offended by your Neanderthal tactics."

"Did it get you to listen to me in a potentially dangerous situation?"

"It got my attention. But I think hearing me out, and the promise to give me fifteen minutes of your time, is what ensured my cooperation."

"So, I'm a Neanderthal and you're crazy. Makes me think we should go out sometime. People would talk."

"Probably not in the way you think." Captain Good Guy and the eccentric bad girl? People would definitely talk…about her ruining his life or corrupting his heroic ways. Amy smiled. "Good night, Mark Taylor. I'm glad I met you."

He caught her hand when she reached the top step. "I was serious about the date thing. When you're ready. After you've had the time you need to grieve."

Bless his think-the-best-of-everyone heart.

That was why he thought she was refusing him? She should have set him straight immediately, but he was giving her time and space. And he wasn't professing insta-love or asking her for anything but an evening of her time. Plus, she really did like the guy...even when he was telling her what to do. Or asking questions. And his face wasn't the only interesting thing about him. She wanted to know more about the dark secrets hidden beneath his friendly exterior. She understood a lot about the differences between what she felt and what she showed the world, too. And how exactly was a woman supposed to resist those smoky blue puppy-dog eyes looking up at her?

"Give me your phone." After he pulled it from the clip on his belt, she typed in her number and the nickname *Red*. "Call or text me sometime."

"I will." When she handed him her cell, he typed in his number and the words *Fire Man*. "So you know it's me." He tucked his phone back onto his belt. "You take care of yourself. No more running *toward* the fire, okay? That's my job."

When Amy stepped onto the porch, the front door opened. The man she now knew to be Mark's father, Gideon Taylor, stepped out, blocking her path. Detectives Beck and Carson flanked him on either side. This couldn't be good. Amy bristled, straightening to every inch of height she possessed and raising her invisible defenses.

Then Dale O'Brien slipped out the door behind

them, his self-satisfied smile curling around the matchstick he chewed between his teeth. Amy glanced behind her, too late spotting the white O'Brien Construction pickup parked in the shadows beyond the lights of the house, behind all the official vehicles lining her driveway. How had she missed seeing him here? Because she'd been too distracted by grief and Captain Good Guy to realize she needed to be protecting herself.

This *so* couldn't be good.

"Miss Hall?" The gravitas in Gideon Taylor's voice demanded her attention. She faced him again, feeling outnumbered, outsmarted and under attack as the three people with badges and that crud O'Brien all studied her.

"What is it, Dad?"

Amy jumped at the weight of Mark Taylor's hand settling at the small of her back. While she appreciated his support, she doubted it would last.

"Son." Gideon acknowledged Mark before returning his gaze to her. "Miss Hall, I'm the chief arson investigator for the KCFD. Our records indicate that we've been out here before investigating suspicious events on your property."

Her gaze immediately shot to the *helpful citizen* who had no doubt reported her. Dale O'Brien would do anything to get her and her gran booted off this property—even take advantage of her vulnerability on the day her best friend had been murdered.

Unless he'd had something to do with that murder? Was the man so desperate to build his Copper Lake empire that he'd kill an innocent woman to set her up like this?

"What did you do, O'Brien?" she accused, letting the anger coursing through her chase away the chill she'd felt a moment ago. She shimmied away from Mark's touch and lifted her gaze back to Deputy Chief Taylor. "It's not what you think, sir."

"Seems pretty straightforward to me." He pointed to the burned-out house down by the lake. That meant O'Brien had told him about the firepit and stables behind the house, too. "You were accused of setting fires."

Chapter Six

Mark stretched out on his bunk at the station house, but it was too early to try to sleep. He'd done his duty by the beef stew and home-baked bread his Station 13 captain, Kyle Redding, had prepared for dinner. But he'd barely tasted it, despite the warm, homey smells that had filled the station house while they'd been washing down the rig, checking hoses and stowing gear. He'd joined his brother Matt for a workout in the house's weight room but had excused himself from an invitation to join some of the men and women he served with for a couple of hands of toothpick poker. Now the sun was setting, the city was quiet, and he had no other reason to put off reading the text he'd received from Amy Hall.

He pulled up the message.

Another rejection.

His breath seeped out on a sigh of disappointment. But he wasn't surprised. He wondered how long he should chase this chemistry he'd felt with the leggy redhead. He wondered how long the image of her crying in her studio behind her welder's mask, hiding away where the chaos couldn't reach her so she could grieve alone, would stay with him.

His instinct had been to take her in his arms, just like he had up on the hill with the burned-out shed where she'd discovered her friend's body. She'd fit against him like two pieces of a puzzle locking together. The woman had curves in all the right places. Yet he could tell she was fit, based on the endurance she'd shown running those Missouri hills. She had hair like wildfire and freckled alabaster skin. She was immensely talented, worked like a badass with power tools and fire, and had a beautiful mouth that could irritate, commiserate and make him laugh. And damn, he wanted to kiss that mouth.

He'd never met anyone like her. He'd never felt this instant, intense draw to another woman before. He wasn't a player, but he had enough experience to know that the attraction was mutual.

But Amy Hall had keeping him at arm's length down to an art form. He didn't need to be a rocket scientist to understand that she was used to handling whatever she needed to on her own.

So, he'd respected her need for space a whole twenty-four hours before calling to leave a voice mail. He'd wanted to make sure she and her grandmother were all right, remind her that his dad was a thorough, but fair, investigator who knew the difference between arson convictions and alleged suspicions that hadn't been proved. And he'd wanted to apologize for Dale O'Brien being such a dickwad to raise those suspicions about her in the first place.

Yes, there'd been two fires on her property before the wildfire that day. One, she confessed to starting when she'd been burning something in the horse paddock and the fire had gotten out of hand. He'd checked the records himself. Amy had been the one to call 9-1-1 that day to contain the accidental fire.

The one at the old foreman's house was still under investigation. And though Dale O'Brien had hinted that she was responsible for setting that one, too, there was no hard evidence to indicate she'd had anything to do with it. Her denial and his loathing for O'Brien had been good enough for Mark to believe her.

But the woman was still hiding something. Something that made him all the more eager to get to know her better, that made him ache to hold her and listen or do whatever was necessary to bring a smile back to that beautiful mouth and chase the wary distrust from her eyes.

So, for two weeks, he'd kept the conversations between them light and safe and fun, getting to know the little things about her before he pushed for the something more he thought could be really, really good between them.

After that first terse We're good. Thanks! reply, he'd waited another twenty-four hours to ask what she charged for one of her pendants or sculptures. How long it took her to create her art. Where did she get her ideas? What was her favorite food? Did she listen to country, rock or classical music? In turn, she'd gotten him to reveal he was a Chiefs football fan. That yes, he'd been to the Nelson-Atkins Museum and Art Gallery—with a school group—and the suits of medieval armor were his favorite display. And that he preferred his grandmother's fried catfish over sushi any day.

Mark had given it a full week before asking her out.

It felt like flirting, reading all the clever ways Amy could say no to his invitations to coffee or lunch or browsing one of the big chain outdoorsman stores in the city before having dinner at the attached Islamorada restaurant. This evening's answer was no different.

In some parts of the world, they call this harassment, Fire Man. ;)

Mark texted right back. In other parts of the world, they say that persistence wins the race.

Amy's reply was accompanied by an eye-rolling emoji. And what race would that be?

The one where you finally say you'll give in to our heat-of-the-moment, opposites-attracting thing and go out with me.

You're never going to let me forget those words, are you, she answered. I can't see you tonight. I've got a university thing with Jocelyn's parents. Sort of a wake for coworkers, profs and students who couldn't get to Nebraska for the funeral. They're making a donation to Williams U in Joss's name. Strictly froufrou event. Speeches, canapés and cocktails. I've been forced to put on a dress and heels.

He closed his eyes, having no problem imagining how killer her legs would look in a getup like that, before typing a response. Need an escort? he offered. I look good in a tux.

Mark smiled at her reply. I bet you do. But there's nary a fried catfish on any of these buffet tables, so I don't know what you'd eat. She'd been paying attention to the little details of their conversations as much as he had. Besides, aren't you at work?

He answered the truth. Yes. But I'd skip out to be your arm candy.

Two minutes passed before she sent a reply.

You're trying to rescue me again. You'd let Kansas City burn just so I don't have to go to this shindig alone?

Alone. There it was again. The thing about Amy Hall that kept nagging at him. She didn't seem to mind chatting, as long as he kept his distance. Based on her responses to his texts, he didn't believe it was him she had an aversion to. Just the idea of dating or relationships, in general. Why on earth was she so determined to be alone?

What had happened in her life to make her think that facing adversity by herself—with just her grandmother for backup—was her safest bet? Was it Mark's relationship to the man who was investigating the arson fires on her property that made her so cautious of doing more than play text tag with him? Was there something going on in her life that was forcing her to be distrustful of a man's interest in her? An image of the portly contractor with the misogynistic attitude toward his mother and Amy came to mind. He really didn't like that guy.

Probably shouldn't. But let's make plans for tomorrow after my shift, ok? I promise, jeans will be the dress code.

She asked, What did you have in mind?
Mark swung his legs over the edge of the bunk

and sat up straight in anticipation. It was the closest response to even a *maybe* he'd gotten since they'd started these daily text chats. He had to give the right answer.

How about you and me talking face-to-face? Let's go for a walk. I'll bring the water bottles and you bring the sunscreen.

Her reply wasn't what he'd expected. Could we go back out to the shed where we found Jocelyn? Detective Beck said they took down the crime scene tape earlier today. No sign of Joss's laptop or even her backpack anywhere.

Mark frowned. Doesn't that place have bad memories for you?

I need answers, Mark. Not Fire Man. Not a joke. I'll go out there on my own if I have to. But I'd rather you came with me. You can tell me what you know about the fire. Help me sort through the debris. Maybe your dad and the police missed something.

Tension knotted at the back of Mark's neck. Her friend had met a killer at that shed, or somewhere close by. She'd been alone, too. No one was in custody for the crimes. Beyond Dale O'Brien, he wasn't even sure who the suspects were that KCPD had been investigating. Besides the awful memories of Jocelyn Brunt's murder, who knew what or who Amy would be facing out there in the remote hills behind her house. No culprit would appreciate a shapely redhead pawing through his business, trying to uncover his identity.

Do NOT go out there by yourself. We don't know who's setting those fires or who killed your friend. He waited a whole minute with no response. Red? No reply. Be safe. I will go with you. I'll call as soon as I get off tomorrow. Wait for me. Tell me you won't investigate any of this on your own. Amy?

Five minutes without any answer and he dialed her number. But when it went straight to voice mail, he got up and paced the length of the bunk room. Either she'd turned her phone off because of the reception, she was ignoring him or he was an absolute fool for worrying about her like this. He stopped at the second-floor window overlooking the landscaping and street in front of the station house. The streetlamps were coming on, telling him the hour was getting late. Still, there were steady lines of traffic moving in both directions, thanks to their location just off the interstate near several restaurants, hotels and suburban neighborhoods.

There were so many people in Kansas City. Probably a lot of people at that hoity-toity university event. Lots of people outside this window. Why wouldn't Amy let him in? Let him be her friend. Let him be something more? He'd always had family around to help him through tough times. He'd always had his real brothers and his brothers at Firehouse 13 to back him up when he needed to take a risk.

Mark pocketed his phone before the frustration building inside him made him sling it across the bunk room. He pounded his fist against the window frame when he couldn't shut off his concern and pulled out his phone to text one last message to Amy. Just let me know you're safe. Ok? A thumbs-up will get me off your back tonight. I promise.

"What did that window ever do to you?" Mark was still waiting for an answer when his brother Matt entered the bunk room. Matt sat on his bunk, stretching his long legs out in front of him. "I'm supposed to be the quiet one. But you're making me look like a regular social butterfly tonight. Thinking about Grandpa again?"

Nope. But he should have been. Mark squeezed his eyes shut against the lousy job he was doing taking care of people lately. He scraped his palm over the top of his hair and blanked the emotion from his face before turning to face his brother. He held up his phone in explanation before stuffing it into the pocket of his BDUs. "Just waiting for somebody to call me back."

Matt picked up a car magazine and flipped through the pages, his tone deceptively indifferent. "It's *her*, then. The redhead?"

No sense denying it. What Matt Taylor lacked in verbosity, he more than made up for in observation skills. Big Brother never missed a trick.

"Her name's Amy." Mark strolled back to his bunk to sit across from Matt. "We've been, um, getting acquainted since that day we got called in on the wildfire."

"Uh-huh."

Mark interpreted that as *I'm interested enough. Keep talking.* "Dad confirmed that there's been three suspicious fires on her property. The first one Amy admitted to—she called 9-1-1 herself. She was burning some trash in a homemade firepit that got out of hand. A couple of weeks after that, she lost a rental property, then another storage shed in the wildfire—the one where we discovered her friend's body. Dad says those last two fires were deliberately set." Matt didn't look up from his magazine, but Mark knew that didn't mean he wasn't listening. "Now she wants to go exploring and solve the crimes by herself. Two fires are a coincidence. Three fires and a murder mean somebody's really pissed off." Mark waited for some flicker of a response in his brother's brown eyes. Could he not see what the problem was? "How do I convince her she isn't safe?"

Matt lowered the magazine to his lap and met Mark's gaze. "You think someone's targeting her with those fires?"

"Dale O'Brien wants her and her grandmother

off that land. If they won't sell, could be he's trying to burn them out."

Matt nodded and dropped his attention back to the article he was reading. "O'Brien was only too happy to let Dad know that she was accused of setting at least one of those fires. That guy is a real piece of work."

"He's probably the one who reported her."

Matt's grunt was as good as an agreement.

"Since she admitted to setting the bonfire in the firepit, she was the first suspect they looked at. She doesn't trust the police. Or Dad. So, she's investigating on her own."

"Sounds risky."

Mark pushed to his feet and paced toward the windows again. "Maybe it's not my place to worry, but I've never seen anyone with less backup than that woman has. I keep asking her out and she keeps putting me off. And the hell of it is, I think she likes me. Maybe she doesn't trust me enough to tell me what's really going on with her. Maybe she thinks I'm just trying to get close to her so I can report to Dad. I've been up-front with her that if I learn anything, I'd have to share it, but that's not why I want to see her."

"She's really gotten under your skin." Matt tossed the magazine aside. "Why are you trying to get close to her? You think you're going to lose somebody else on your watch?"

"It's more than that. She needs somebody, Matt." *I want her to need me.*

"You sure you're not making up a threat that isn't there, so you can get closer to her?"

Mark muttered a curse and shook his head. "I am not making this up. At least, I don't think I am. There's something dangerous surrounding Amy Hall. I think she needs help. But she's too proud, or too scared, to ask for it. So, I'm offering."

"Grandpa would tell you to trust your gut. You think she needs help? Then do something about it." Matt Taylor was a big reflection in the window as he walked up behind Mark and rested a hand on his shoulder. "But if this is just about you needing to save somebody because you feel guilty about Grandpa, let it go. The only one who blames you for Grandpa's heart attack is you."

Mark shrugged off his brother's touch. "Amy and I have been talking or texting every day. And it's not just me being all stalkerish. She contacts me as often as I do her. We've got a connection. She's funny. And smart. She thinks *I'm* funny."

"Oh, well, now I know there's something wrong with her."

Turning, Mark smacked Matt in the arm. "Maybe you've got no interest in a relationship, but I think we could be something if she'd give us a chance."

"What makes you think I've got no interest—?"

"I'm fine with going slow, if that's what she needs. But I don't want to lose the possibility of being with her because she's too pigheaded to listen to reason."

Bracing his hands at his waist, Matt puffed up to a size that intimidated most men. But that only made Mark match his stance. He knew his brother too well to be intimidated by whatever salient point he suddenly wanted to make. "Amy's not the only woman trouble you have."

"Huh?"

"At Sunday dinner, Grandma Martha asked why you weren't there. She knew you weren't working because I was there." Matt crossed his arms over his chest and glared. "She thinks you're avoiding her."

"There were plenty of people there with her to christen the new house, right?"

"We were all there. Every uncle, every aunt, every cousin. So, it stuck out that you were missing."

"Grandpa is the one who's missing, Matt. I…" Mark turned to the window and looked down into the night. He hated that he'd caused Grandma Martha any pain. "I let the man she loves die. Why would she want me around to remind her of that?"

Matt's chest expanded as though he was about to light into Mark. But the fire alarm sounded, ending whatever butt-chewing session he'd been about to receive. Personal matters took a back seat as the call to duty rang through the building and the brothers Taylor answered.

"Let's move it, Thirteen," Captain Redding called over the intercom as Mark and Matt jogged to the stairs. "Structure fire, fully engulfed. All trucks are rolling."

"We'll finish this conversation later," Matt announced as they hurried to their gear lockers. "And put the redhead out of your mind for now, too, bro. I don't want to be saving your butt because you're thinking about a woman instead of the call."

Mark gave Matt a curt nod and picked up his gear, letting his training move him through the steps he needed to perform. He stepped into his turnout pants and boots and grabbed his coat and helmet before climbing up to his position behind the driver's seat of the first engine truck. Mark leaned forward as Matt settled behind the wheel and started the engine. "Where are we headed, Cap?"

Captain Redding settled into the seat across from Matt and punched the address into the engine's GPS system. "Copper Lake."

The adrenaline pumping through Mark's veins skidded to a halt as recognition hit, filling him with dread. "That's where Amy lives."

"Who's Amy?" the captain asked.

"A friend." A friend who didn't need more of

this kind of trouble. Mark sank back into his seat before meeting his brother's stoic gaze in the rear-view mirror. "You still think I'm making up a reason to rescue her?"

Chapter Seven

Amy glanced down at the last text Mark had sent her and considered sending him a thumbs-up, so that he would stop worrying. She wasn't reckless enough to search through the hills of her grandmother's farm at this time of night on her own.

But as a tipsy guest jostled her without apologizing at the reception's free bar, she couldn't exactly assure him that she felt okay. Her toes were pinched to the point of numbness in these high heels, and her patience had been pinched even further. She'd already stayed an hour longer than she'd intended. She'd traded hugs with Jocelyn's parents, shaken hands with the Dean of Arts & Science, who'd asked if she was considering reapplying for graduate school, and applauded speeches by the dean, Jocelyn's parents and the supervising professor for Jocelyn's doctoral project.

As the man who'd bumped her brushed past her again, eager to greet a friend, Amy stepped up to the bar and placed her order. "I'd like a cola. Whatever you have with caffeine. Just give me the can. I don't need a glass. And a bottle of water."

She looked over her shoulder to the blond man in the crumpled black tux and dangling bow tie who sat with his head in his hands near the exit door. Derek Roland was the only reason she was still here. When she found him out in the parking lot, trying to unlock his car with his apartment key, she'd offered to call a car for him. With vomit staining his shoes and the hem of his trousers, he clearly was in no shape to drive. But then he'd fallen onto her, trapping her against the car and swallowing her in an uncomfortable hug as he wept onto her shoulder.

Deciding Derek was too drunk and despondent to be left to his own devices for any length of time, Amy had helped him back inside with the intent of sobering him up before he went home.

Unlike her drunk, dramatic friend there, Mark Taylor probably looked freakin' hot in a tuxedo. Not that a firefighter's uniform or sweaty T-shirt had done him any injustice. Plus, he'd be more entertaining. She could certainly use a few laughs after the strain of smiling all evening, pretending she was fine being back on the campus that had once been her beloved home. She had a feeling that Mark wouldn't have gotten so stinking drunk and become a burden to her tonight, either.

He was too considerate for that. He would have realized that she was grieving, too. He wouldn't have made tonight all about him.

Giving in to the temptation of connecting with Mark again, Amy pulled out her phone and re-read the draft of the text she'd typed while she'd been waiting in line for caffeine.

I changed my mind. Could I see you tonight? I could use a friendly, interesting face. Are you at the station house? Tuxedo is optional. ;)

"Ma'am?" The bartender popped the tab on the cola and set it in front of her. "Your drinks?"

"Thanks." Amy sent the text before she could question the wisdom of getting closer to Mark, dropped some money into the tip jar, and wove her way through the groupings and conversations to Derek. "Feeling any better?" she asked as she sat down across from him. She set the cola in front of him and opened the water for herself. "Here. Drink as much of that as you can. I figured you could manage it better than a cup of coffee."

At least the wailing had stopped. But his eyes were red and puffy when he leaned back in his chair. He raked his fingers through his shaggy hair, surveying the dwindling crowd before settling his bleary gaze on her. "Why are you being so good to me, Amy? I don't deserve it."

Maybe not. Derek wasn't the only one grieving in this room or sharing fond memories of Jocelyn and celebrating her work and her life. But he was the only one who'd made a noisy, public display of his heartbreak, to the point that his fellow grad students and professors had turned away from the emotional drain he imposed on them.

As far as Amy was concerned, she'd stuck by him because of Jocelyn. She owed her friend that much, to take care of the man she'd left behind. Joss would have done the same. Otherwise, these killer shoes would be off, and she'd be home in bed or in her studio.

Or maybe she'd give in to the foolish urge to see Mark Taylor in person again. To feel his soothing touch. To laugh at his goofy humor. To lean on him like the pillar of strength that he was.

Right now, she had no one to lean on but herself.

"You've had too much to drink. And you're grieving. It's hard to manage one when you're dealing with the other." Amy pushed the can toward him. "Drink up. I'm calling that car for you once you sober up a little more. I don't want you barfing again in the back seat."

He chuckled and reached for the cola, downing a long drink before reaching across the table to capture her hand in his tight grip. "I've ruined the party for you. I'm sorry."

Amy couldn't help but compare his crushing grip to the gentle strength of Mark's hand. With Mark, she could have pulled away if she'd wanted. She tugged against Derek's hand. A remembered panic from Preston's attack bubbled through her blood. Maybe he was too inebriated to realize he was hurting her. "Derek, let go," she ordered. If anything, his grip on her tightened, nearly snapping her wrist. "Let. Go."

His drunken haze seemed to vanish for a split second, and his green eyes zeroed in on hers before his grip suddenly popped open and he raised his hands in mock surrender. "Sorry. Don't know my own strength, I guess. Did I hurt you?"

Amy assessed the thumbprint that would show up as a bruise on her fair skin within the hour. But out loud, she answered, "Nothing that needs a doctor. Just be more careful next time."

He nodded and took another long drink of cola. "I really have ruined your night."

"I haven't been in much of a party mood anyway, lately," she confessed. "I wanted to be here to support Joss's mom and dad. But, whenever you're feeling up to it, I am ready to head for home."

"Me, too." He downed the rest of his soda in one final chug. At least he covered his mouth when a noisy belch followed. As his foul alcohol breath carried across the table, Amy subtly rubbed the hand he'd crushed in her lap. Remembering the force of Preston Worth's attack was much harder to erase. His hand had been at her throat. His fists had been everywhere. And then there'd been that horrible fall. "You're so much stronger about all this than I am."

No. She was just a survivor. That was what she was good at.

"We all grieve differently." Amy offered the platitude before standing and circling around to link her hand in the crook of Derek's elbow and pull him to his feet. "Come on. A walk in the fresh air will do you some good, too."

"Just give me my keys and I'll go home."

"You're not driving anywhere. Now walk."

They reached the edge of the parking lot before she stopped and pulled her phone from her purse to call a car service. She spared a moment of disappointment when she saw that Mark hadn't answered her text. Was this how he felt when she got too worried about how emotionally involved she was getting and put off replying? She couldn't blame him for ignoring her and giving her a taste of her own medicine. Or was he on a call with his team? Was worrying about him battling a fire or dealing with a dangerous accident any easier than feeling guilty or hurt by the absence of any contact with him?

Wow. Where was her head these days, when her hopes and sorrows centered around whether or not Mark connected with her?

"Amy?" She quickly scrolled off her text messages when Derek bumped her arm. He was sobering up, but not as quickly as she'd like. "Wish I could get out of this damn monkey suit. Especially with the…" He stumbled against her as he looked down at his soiled shoes. "You know."

Irritation warred with pity. If she didn't believe this sad sack's love for Jocelyn was genuine, the pity might not have won. With a weary huff, Amy linked her arm through Derek's and turned him toward the agricultural sciences building. "Do you have a change of clothes at your office?"

He nodded.

"Then let's go there." Since Derek's university ID was on his key chain, she had no trouble leading him past the building's nighttime security guard and heading to his tiny office at the top of the stairs.

Once there, Derek took his bag of running gear to the bathroom down the hall and changed. Amy wished she still had an office on campus and a pair of tennis shoes or flip-flops to change into, too. But since she suspected she'd never get her swollen feet wedged inside these heels again for the drive home, she sat in the lone chair behind Derek's messy desk and waited to make sure he didn't pass out somewhere between the bathroom and loading him into the car that would take him home.

As emotionally exhausted as she was, her mind wandered. Before she fully realized what she was doing, Amy was tidying up the stack of student essay books spread across his blotter and sticking stray pens, paper clips and sticky-note pads into the desk drawer with other office supplies. She reached into her purse for a tissue to dust off the dingy keyboard and screen of his laptop, and smiled when she discovered the black cotton bandanna Mark had given her the night Jocelyn had died. Even when she couldn't reach the firefighter who had wormed his way into nearly every thought, this old-fashioned token of his Captain Good Guy persona warmed her heart and eased some of the stress of the evening.

Feeling an uncharacteristic urge of sentimentality, Amy twisted the bandanna into a long skein and tied it around her wrist. Maybe the time had come for her to admit she had feelings for Mark Taylor, that she wanted to be more than just texting buddies. That one of these days, she was going to have to sit him down and tell him all her twisted past and current hang-ups and see if he was still interested in turning their daily flirtations into something more serious.

Feeling a little lighter now that she'd admitted those feelings and was considering the risk of taking on a relationship again, starting with that date Mark kept teasing her about, Amy went back to cleaning Derek's desk. She found the tissue she'd been looking for and dusted off the screen and keyboard before closing the university-issued laptop and straightening it on the corner of the blotter.

And then she saw the second laptop hiding beneath a hodgepodge of maps and file folders. She almost called down the hall to Derek to ask what he'd done to rate two laptops, or if he'd been careless enough to lose one in this mess and had requested a replacement, when she got a better look at the second laptop.

"What is…?" She fingered the sticky bits of fuzz and glue on the laptop's outside cover where someone had peeled off a sticker. Not just any sticker, but one with the nearly imperceptible outline of two initials…a *J* and a *B. Jocelyn Brunt.*

Amy unplugged the laptop and flipped it over to find the remnants of another familiar sticker. Although the shredded bits of glue and plastic gave no indication to what had once been there, the location was exactly where Joss had put the emblem of a female superhero who'd inspired her.

Had the air-conditioning kicked on in the small office? Or was the chill racing down Amy's spine confirmation that Derek had his hands on something he shouldn't?

Amy hugged the laptop to her chest and stood as Derek leaned against the door frame. "I'm as ready as I can be…" When he saw what was in her arms, when he saw her crossing toward him with a purpose, Derek straightened. "What are you doing?" He dropped his tuxedo jacket and slacks on the worktable beside him. "Are you going through my things?"

"This isn't *your* thing." If possible, he turned even paler and looked like he might be sick again. But Amy's sympathy had left the building. "You know damn well this is Jocelyn's. Where did you get it? How long have you had it? You do know the police are looking for it, right?"

"I know." He sagged against the door frame. "I wasn't finished with it."

He wasn't *finished*? He'd known its location for two weeks and hadn't said anything? "Damn it, Derek. The police think this could be key to finding Jocelyn's killer. And you…?" Amy muttered a curse and pushed him out of her way, heading for the stairs. "I'm turning this over to the police. And I'm telling them exactly where I found it."

"She left it in my apartment the night before she died."

Amy spun around to face him. "She left it? Jocelyn never went anywhere without this." She frowned as another thought registered. Maybe a better question was, *She stayed the night with you?*

Wait. Amy eyed her position at the top of the stairs and felt the yawning expanse down to the first floor ripple through her vision like a chimera of heat. Blinking away the dizzying sensation, she moved to the side, so she wasn't in such a vulnerable position to an impulsive shove down to the first floor as Derek shuffled toward her. Maybe the smartest question she could ask was, "Did you have anything to do with Joss's murder?"

"What?" Derek's hands shot up in surrender and he drifted back a step. "No. God, no. I loved her."

She knew better than most that love didn't necessarily mean violence couldn't also be part of a relationship. "Tell me exactly how you got this," she ordered, wondering if she was having this conversation with Jocelyn's killer. Maybe she should get her phone out and call Detective Beck. No, her key chain with the canister of pepper spray was a better option right now. Amy pulled her keys out of her purse and put her finger on the button, showing Derek that she wasn't going to be afraid of him. She wasn't going to leave without answers, either. "Tell me about the night before Jocelyn died."

Derek lowered his hands and drifted back to the door frame, as if he needed its support to stand. "Joss and I spent some time together that last week. She told me you said she should put herself first, that she should do what was right for her." His mouth tightened into a grim line as though he hadn't appreciated that advice. "Maybe she loved me more than you thought she did. She came over to talk and…things heated up."

"Are you talking breakup sex?"

"No!" For a man who was two blinks away from passing out, Derek was suddenly loud and lunging toward her. Amy aimed the pepper spray, but the walls must have whirled around his vision because he stumbled back into the doorway, clinging to the frame to keep himself upright. He might be less of a threat, but the bile toward her was still there. "I'm talking about two-people-who-are-meant-to-be-together kind of sex. I needed to know that she still loved me. I wanted her to know that once her degree was done, I would be there for her."

Yeah, yeah. True love. Emotional blackmail. Amy wasn't interested. "Tell me about the laptop."

"I woke up before her the next morning, the day she died." He shook his head and tears filled his eyes. "I just wanted some confirmation of her findings to fact-check against my own dissertation. But then she was awake…but I hadn't found the information I needed…and I didn't want her to think that was the reason I'd slept with her… so I hid it. When she didn't find it in her bag, I suggested that she left it at your place. Or in her equipment shed. Later that day—I knew she'd been evacuated because of the fire—I was driving the laptop back to your place to stick it in her room when you called me."

"You son of a bitch. You can't *use* somebody and love her at the same time."

Derek sank down against the wall until he was sitting on the floor and blubbering again. But this wasn't grief. It was guilt. Despair. "Don't you see what I've done? She must have driven out to the shed that morning looking for her laptop. I sent her to her death. She wouldn't have been there if it wasn't for me."

Could his lame story be true? Or was he trying to give himself some kind of alibi? Despite his obvious distress, Amy was done offering comfort. "You won't get any more sympathy from me tonight. You sure you didn't have an argument with her over stealing her research? Maybe you got a little rough?"

"And took her out to your place to hide the body? I'm not that gnarly old professor who beat on you!" His words struck Amy like a slap across the face. Maybe that had been his intention, his way of getting her to back off. He scraped his palm over his jaw, shaking his head. "I'm sorry, Amy. I didn't mean that. I blame the whiskey."

As he straightened his legs across the floor in front of him, apparently too weak to stand, Amy explained just how damning his words had sounded. "Derek. When you're drunk, or overly emotional, it's not a stretch to see how lashing out with words can become lashing out with a fist or whatever object is close at hand." She inhaled a steadying breath to calm her own emotions and remind herself that she was the sober one here. "I have to tell the police what you said to me. You need to call them tomorrow when you're clear-headed and tell them exactly what you told me."

"I didn't kill her."

"That's not for me to determine. But you may have been the last person to see her before her killer did. You had her laptop and everything she was working on. If you don't call KCPD tomorrow, I will send the detectives to your apartment."

"I swear, leaving my bed that morning was the last time I saw Joss before she was gone." Derek raked his fingers through his hair. Every strand fell right back into place, reminding her of the temptation of Mark Taylor's wayward hair and where she'd rather be.

Since Derek's legs were apparently jelly right now, and she was out of arm's reach, Amy felt it was safe to venture to the top of the stairs again. "I'll call a car to pick you up in twenty minutes. Meet it out front. I'll leave your keys with the security guard, so you don't try to drive yourself and do damage to anyone else."

"Damage? Amy, I didn't mean to hurt you—"

"Good night."

Amy explained the situation to the security guard at the front desk, tucked the laptop under her arm and headed outside. She'd call Detective Beck and drop it off at North Precinct headquarters in the morning, if the woman wasn't on duty tonight. She hurried across campus to the alumni center parking lot where she'd left her truck. Armed with pepper spray and a pair of heels she wasn't afraid to use as a weapon, she was hyperaware of someone watching her, following closely enough to keep her in sight without being seen. Just like the night of Jocelyn's death, when goose bumps had prickled up her spine, Amy sensed that she'd become the focus of someone's curiosity. Or obsession. Or rage.

She stopped once, turned, wondering if Derek had gotten past the security guard and was trying to see if she would call 9-1-1 and report him for being in possession of key evidence. But she saw no one suspicious, nothing unusual. There was a group of older teens, probably freshmen here for some kind of orientation or camp, moving in a loud, laughing pack from the fine arts building over to one of the fast-food places in the student union. But no Derek. No other adults on the sidewalks. No slow-moving car tracking her across campus.

Although the group of young students had come from the music wing of the fine arts building, she lifted her gaze to the windows of the art department where she'd once had a tiny office. Where she'd taken numerous classes and posed in Preston Worth's studio. Preston no longer worked at the university, but there was a light on in the window that used to be his office. A shadow moved behind the blinds and disappeared. Amy gasped for a breath. It was probably just the cleaning crew at this time of night. Some other professor worked in that office now. Preston had served his time and moved to a remote town in Montana where he taught at a community college and probably had some other impressionable young student he was preying upon. The attorney who'd handled Amy's case kept tabs on him. She would let Amy know if he was anywhere back in Kansas City. Plus, he was persona non grata at Williams University. If he stepped foot on campus, he could be arrested.

So, not Derek. Not Preston. Not anyone she could see. Still, she had a hard time hearing anything beyond the drumbeat of her pulse pounding in her ears.

Amy swallowed her fears and turned away from the window. She was just projecting her imagination after the vile things Derek had said tonight and done to Jocelyn. "I'm fine," she whispered out loud, hurrying her pace. "Just get to the truck and you'll be fine."

Once she reached her truck without anyone showing his face or accosting her, Amy didn't waste any time climbing inside and locking the doors. She tossed the laptop and her purse on the seat beside her and started the engine, racing out of the parking lot in an effort to put Derek and her cruel imagination behind her as quickly as possible.

At the first stoplight, she exhaled a breath she'd

been holding for far too long and pulled out her phone to text Mark. Was he busy at work? Had she pushed him away so many times that he didn't believe she wanted to see him?

She typed quickly before she lost her nerve and denied herself what she wanted, what she was afraid she needed. I'm sorry I gave you any reason to doubt my interest. I DO want to see you. I could use some friendly Captain Good Guy vibes right about now. Wish you'd answer. I'm stopping by tonight if that's ok.

Amy sent the message and had just typed in a search for the street address for Fire Station 13 when her phone rang. A moment's excitement, expecting to see Mark's name and hear his voice, evaporated in an instant when she saw her grandmother's name instead. What was Comfort Hall still doing up at this hour?

Amy instantly answered. "Gran? I know I'm running later than I said, but—"

"Amy. Sweetheart. You need to come home. Right now."

"What's wrong?" The light changed, and the car behind her honked. Amy steered her truck toward the highway and home, instead of turning toward Firehouse 13. "Are you all right? Is it your blood pressure? Did you take your pills today?"

"Of course I did. I'm fine. It's not me."

Then what warranted this hushed urgency? "What's going on?"

"I've already called the authorities."

Not reassuring. She pressed harder on the accelerator. Something was seriously wrong. "Authorities? Gran?"

"You know the rental house those two road workers shared?"

"Yes?"

"It's on fire."

Chapter Eight

Fortunately, the highway patrol wasn't out in force to clock Amy flying down the interstate toward home.

Despite the urge to call her grandmother again, she resolutely kept both hands on the wheel, slowing down only when she reached the turnoff to Copper Lake. She sped past the older suburban neighborhood, gas stations and convenience stores near the highway exit, then wound through the hills and trees beyond.

"Oh, no." Once she left the lights of civilization behind her, Amy spotted the smoke, a darker shade of black roiling up above the horizon into the night sky and blotting out the familiar stars. She tried to confirm the location of the fire, logically knowing it was too far down in the next valley to be her grandmother's house. But it was still too close. And there'd been too many fires. Amy didn't breathe any deeper or ease her concern over her lone surviving family member until the hills opened onto Copper Lake itself and she saw the spotlights and swirling warning lights of several fire engines silhouetting the rental house on the north side of the lake.

She drove through the Copper Lake subdivision and was sickened to see Dale O'Brien's white truck parked in front of his office trailer. Why was he always around whenever trouble screwed with her life these days? Every light in the trailer was on, as though he was working through all the commotion without a care that his neighbors' property and lives were in danger. Several of his workers stood around their vehicles, watching the excitement and using their phones to record the devastation across the lake. With no sidewalks yet, the men were standing in the middle of the road, forcing Amy to slow her truck to a crawl to move safely past them.

"Miss Amy!" someone shouted. Amy glanced out the passenger window to see Richie Sterling's sunburned cheeks puffed up like apples as he beamed a smile and waved. "Glad to see you're okay."

"Thanks." Automatically, Amy raised her hand in a wave. Judging by their state of dress and the tool belts a few still wore, the construction workers had been here since the end of their workday. She stepped on the brake, rolled down the passenger-side window and waved Richie over. She hated to think these men were hanging around because they saw the destruction of her property and the threat to her tiny family as some kind of morbid entertainment, like drivers who stopped to study the aftermath of a car wreck. "What are you all still doing here? I didn't see any roads blocked off. Is the fire department keeping you here for a reason?"

Brad Frick appeared in the window next to his friend, sticking his beak-like nose into their conversation before Richie could answer. "It's Friday. We're all waitin' for our paycheck." He curled his work-gloved fingers over the bottom of the window, and Amy idly noticed the scrapes and bruises on Richie's hands gripping the door frame beside him. True workman's hands.

What was her fascination with men's hands lately? Brad's were hidden. Richie's damaged. Derek's hand had been crushing and Mark Taylor's strong, yes, but infinitely gentle.

Mark. Amy glanced across the lake to the firefighters battling the flames. She needed to get home. She needed to see Gran. She wanted desperately to talk to Mark.

Wait. These men were waiting for a paycheck late on a Friday night? "Don't any of you have direct deposit?"

Brad muttered something under his breath. "O'Brien says there's something wrong with the computer payroll system. He can't make it work.

So, he's writin' out paper checks. Of course, Richie and me are at the bottom of his list."

Richie nodded. "Yep. No matter what job we do, we're the last to get paid."

"Shut up." Brad elbowed him out of the way. "You got any work for us, Miss Amy? We'd be happy to come out this weekend, or come in early Monday, or stay late, whatever you need."

Wanting this conversation to end and to be on her way right now more than she wanted the two men hanging out at her place with everything else that was going on, Amy halfway agreed. "Once the fire is out, there will probably be some debris that'll need to be hauled away. Of course, KCFD and the investigators will have to clear the scene. Probably not this weekend, but I'll call you as soon as I know anything."

"Appreciate it."

"Here you go, boys." Brad turned away from her truck as Dale O'Brien came out of his trailer, waving a stack of envelopes in his hand. He started calling out names and handing out the paychecks. Once the men grabbed their envelopes, they headed for their trucks and cars, thankfully turning their attention to something besides her family's misfortune across the lake. Before he was done with the checks, O'Brien handed them off to one of the men to finish distributing them and filled up Amy's window before the road ahead cleared and she could drive away. "How's your grandmother?" he asked, as if they'd shared friendly chats like this a hundred times. She couldn't help but notice the pristine manicure on the fingers he drummed against the door. "I hope this latest fire hasn't frightened her."

"Now that your men have cleared the road for me, I intend to find out. But I'm sure she's fine."

And here came the relentless sales pitch. "You know, with that old house gone, that's just one less place for me to clear when I start building over there."

"It's not your land to build on," Amy reminded him.

His belly jiggled as he chuckled. "I'd still give you a fair price, despite the loss of that house devaluing the property."

"Sounds like a great scam. Setting fires to devalue our property so you could scare us away and buy it cheap."

He straightened from the door. "Are you accusing me of something, Crazy Amy?"

Amy's knuckles were white with tension as she shifted the truck into Drive and pulled away. "Good night, Mr. O'Brien."

Amy drove on as quickly as she dared, circling around the lake, feeling soiled somehow, as she did after almost every encounter with the greedy contractor.

She skirted the spinning lights and red-and-gold engines blocking the asphalt road and cut into the ditch, driving straight across the dead grass until she reached her driveway. Once she parked and climbed out, she did an immediate assessment of her surroundings. She spotted her grandmother standing on the front porch in her robe and pajamas. Their neighbor, Gerald Sanders, stood beside her, his arm draped around her shoulders. Her grandmother clasped her hands together like a prayer and blew a kiss to Amy when she stepped out. Amy answered back by blowing a kiss before turning to the fire itself.

Although there was little breeze and the smoke seemed to billow up straight into the night, her eyes stung with the scents of sulfur and ash floating in the air. She clung to the side of her truck as a beam or wall crashed to the floor inside and she heard a noise like the snap of a dozen matchsticks before flames shot up through the roof. There was a thunderous rush of water from the main hose attached to the hydrant, and another, smaller hose, pumping water from one of the engines itself. The man in a white helmet shouted orders, just as Mark's mother had, and others responded.

Her stomach clenched when she saw the *Lucky 13* logo on the sides of every fire engine and knew Mark and the men and women he served with were here. She tried to find him on one of the hoses or stamping out burning embers with dirt and shovels between the burning structure and Gerald Sanders's home. Amy spared a quick glance of panic at Gerald's house. It appeared to be a far enough distance away to be safe unless the firefighters missed one of the embers and it floated onto his roof.

Where was Mark in all this well-orchestrated chaos? Was he safe? Was this another arson fire set by her number one suspect, Dale O'Brien, or some other lunatic with a grudge against her, putting these brave men and women in harm's way? Did that fire monger realize how much she cared about Mark?

Amy waited a few moments longer, hoping to see him and assure herself he was okay. With the dancing shadows, bright lights of the fire and engine lights on their faces or the distortion of their masks the firefighters closest to the blaze wore, it was nearly impossible for her to identify anyone.

The one exception was Mark's brother. Simply put, Matt Taylor was the biggest guy out there. He hauled an ax over his shoulder and reported something to the captain in the white helmet.

The captain shouted his response over the noise. "Tap into the hydrant across the lake if we need it. We'll pump out of the lake itself if we have to. Keep this line going until our men are out."

"Yes, sir." Matt, clearly a second-in-command, whatever that title might be, pointed to two other firefighters and relayed an order that sent them running to move one of the trucks.

Then he turned to Amy, startling her. She flattened her back against the side of the truck. She thought she was staying out of the way. How had he even noticed she was here? But a few long strides brought him to her. Up close, she could see the perspiration and grime marking his face beneath his helmet. His expression was as grim as Mark's was friendly. "We've got it under control. Go up to the house."

He was imposing, yes, but he was a Taylor and Mark had joked about him, so she wasn't afraid. "Where's Mark?" she asked.

Stern stoicism aside, Matt at least had the grace to give her a straight answer. "He and Jackson are doing a room-to-room search to make sure whoever set this didn't get trapped inside."

That aching knot in her stomach intensified as she glanced beyond him to the fire. "He's inside that?"

Since he must have considered that a rhetorical question, he didn't answer. "Your house is a safe distance from the job." The job? He called this life-threatening destruction of a nearly hundred-year-old home that could potentially kill his brother a job? She supposed she had a lot to learn about firefighters. Matt pointed his gloved hand up to the porch where her grandmother and Gerald were watching. "Beyond those front steps is not. Stay with them. Keep them out of harm's way."

His deep-pitched command was not open for

discussion. She wondered if he was simply giving her something to do in an attempt to alleviate the worry that must be etched all over her face, or if he thought she'd be a distraction to Mark. Whatever the reason, Amy nodded. "Thank you for talking to me. Thank you for being here."

Behind Matt, there was a loud crash as the front bay window shattered. Another firefighter cleared the glass and broken frame pieces, and Mark climbed out behind him, carrying a limp body wrapped in a shiny silver blanket in his arms. When they were several yards away from the structure, the two men laid the body on the ground. Mark tugged the mask off his face and shouted, "Medic!"

Although soot and sweat camouflaged his exact expression, there was no mistaking the direction of his gaze, seeking out Matt beside her truck, then darting briefly to her. He nodded an acknowledgment of her presence and she hugged her arms around her waist. The tension in her stomach unknotted a fraction and she knew the silliest urge to either smile or start crying.

Matt's heavy hand dropped to her shoulder, turning her toward the house. "Go."

His touch wasn't much in the way of comfort, yet she found Matt's terse order oddly reassuring. While she was relieved to see that Mark was in one piece, it was frightening to realize that someone had been caught in the fire and was seriously, if not fatally, injured. She hadn't fallen apart when she'd been the object of violence herself, and she wouldn't fall apart now when Mark, his brother and the rest of the Station 13 crew, her grandmother, and that poor victim on the blanket needed her to be strong. "Thank you."

While Matt jogged back into the fray, Mark and two paramedics unwrapped the person he'd rescued, put a breathing mask on the victim's face and began their examination. With a team of paramedics swarming around, it was impossible to identify anything more than charred clothes on the blanket. Meanwhile, Amy finally plucked those painful shoes off her feet, curled her toes into the cool grass and hurried up to the house.

Get out of here. Do something useful. Clearly, she wasn't the one who needed to be rescued tonight, nor did she want to be.

"Amy!" Comfort called to her as Amy ran up the porch steps. The two women wrapped each other up in a hug. "I'm so glad you're safe."

Amy tightened her hold as much as she dared when she felt the coolness of her grandmother's cheek pressed against hers. "I'm glad *you're* safe."

"Isn't this terrible?" Comfort finally pulled away to tighten her robe. She crossed her arms in front of her, rubbing her hands up and down her sleeves. "So many fires in such a short time. These can't all be accidents."

Amy was beginning to wonder if any of them

besides the one she'd set when she'd burned up the last bits of her life with Preston Worth could be accidents. As she draped her arm around her grandmother's shoulders and let the older woman lean against her, she noticed that Gerald was wearing a pair of slippers and a pajama shirt with the jeans and sweater he must have hastily thrown on. Both of them must have been sound asleep when this tragedy started. "Thank you for being here, Gerald. I came home as soon as I heard. I appreciate you staying with Gran. I might not have worried so much if I'd known you were with her." He curled his gnarled fingers around a bar of scaffolding, moving slightly away, yet making no show of leaving. "You discovered the fire?"

"I smelled the smoke. Came up to the house to make sure Comfort was all right." He glanced down at Comfort, then quickly turned his gaze back to the fire, making Amy wonder, not for the first time, if the reclusive older gentleman had a bit of a crush on her grandmother. "Then we saw the flames and she called 9-1-1."

The three of them stood together a few minutes longer, watching KCFD battle the blaze. Thankfully, they seemed to be winning, although Amy was certain it would be a total loss by the time the fire was out. And that poor victim who'd been trapped inside.

Once the paramedics drove away in the ambulance, Comfort reached up to pat Amy's hand.

"What did that firefighter say to you? Was it that nice Mark Taylor you've had your eye on?"

"Gran!" This was hardly the time for match-making, even if she *had* been looking for Mark among the crew from Firehouse 13. "I haven't seen Mark since the last time he was out here."

"But I know you've been texting him on the phone. He makes you laugh. That makes me like him."

"I only saw him briefly," Amy confessed. "I talked to Mark's brother Matt. He said we were safe here."

"Did he say anything about that body…?" Comfort moved her hand to her chest, mindlessly rubbing her hand over her heart. Was her heart racing? Her blood pressure spiking? "No one was living there unless we had a squatter. Who is it? How badly are they hurt?"

"They don't know any of that yet, Gran. Matt told me to make sure the three of us were safe."

"We're not hurt."

Danger aside, Amy didn't like the effect this stress was having on her grandmother's health. "Did you take all your pills today?"

"I'm sure I did. Although, I'd have to check my pillbox."

"I'll do that," Amy offered, hating that her grandmother seemed so fragile tonight. Normally, Comfort Hall was a tough old bird, but Jocelyn's murder and these arson fires seemed to be taking a toll on her. Coming just two years after her husband's death and Amy's life blowing up over her breakup with Preston, it was a lot for a woman Comfort's age—of any age—to deal with. "Why don't you go lie down? Do your breathing exercises or read a book and try to relax. I'll get your blood pressure cuff and we can check your BP, just in case."

Comfort adjusted her glasses on her nose and frowned up at Amy. "I'm worrying you, aren't I?"

"If I didn't love you so much, I wouldn't."

"You don't need this stress any more than I do. It's like Preston all over again." She found Amy's hand and squeezed it. "I want only good things for you. A good man. Happiness." She looked down at the burning house and shook her head. "Not this. I don't want this to be the legacy I leave to you."

"None of this is your fault, Gran." She tightened her hug around Comfort's shoulders. "This is your home. You were born and raised here. You raised Dad here, then me. No one has the right to force you to leave your home."

"If I find out Mr. O'Brien set any one of these fires, I'll be first in line to punch him myself." Amy thought she detected a soft chuckle from Gerald.

Amy found she could smile, too. "That's my girl. You and I are going to be okay."

Comfort reached up to cup Amy's cheek and

smiled. "I am a little tired, dear. You'll tell me when the fire is out? Or if it comes toward the house?"

"Of course."

Then Comfort turned to Mr. Sanders and squeezed his arm. "Thank you for waking me, Gerald. And for staying with me. It's nice to have a man around the place again. But I'll be all right now that Amy is here."

"I wouldn't want to see you get hurt, Comfort." He covered her hand with his own before she released him and headed into the house. Once the door was closed, he nodded to Amy. "I'd better be going."

"Would you like to stay here tonight?" Amy stepped into his path at the edge of the porch, thumbing over her shoulder to the firefighters behind her. "Looks like they'll be working for a while yet."

His white brows knitted together. "It wouldn't be proper."

Matt Taylor had told Amy to take care of these two. And since he'd helped her grandmother tonight, she owed Gerald. "I'm a grown woman. And so is Gran. It's going to be noisy and smell like smoke at your place for a couple of hours yet, if not the rest of the night. Maybe just a cup of coffee? I promise I won't try to make conversation with you."

He snorted a sound that she thought might just

be a laugh. His dark eyes studied her sincerity a moment before he nodded. "Well, I suppose I won't have any water pressure tonight, either." That sounded more like a joke than a complaint. Finally, he nodded again. "I'll take the coffee. Decaf, if you have it."

"It's all Gran drinks anymore." Amy opened the door and let him precede her into the foyer.

Before closing the door, she turned to give the fire one last look, checking every firefighter until she found Mark again. No wonder he hadn't answered her texts. He was busy saving lives. He didn't have time to rescue her tonight, and she shouldn't have wanted him to. She should be stronger than that, strong enough to handle aging grandmothers and fires and Derek Roland and Dale O'Brien and whatever else the world tossed at her.

But it was hard to always be strong. It was lonely, too.

What if she was only imagining a relationship between her and Mark? They hadn't even had that date he kept pestering her about yet. Still, she felt like she knew him. And she couldn't ignore the attraction they shared.

She was setting herself up for heartache by thinking she could trust any man the way she'd mistakenly trusted Preston. But Captain Good Guy and the whole Taylor family seemed like the embodiment of trust. Mark wasn't even hers to worry about. But she did. She'd never forget seeing him burst out of those flames, knowing he'd risked his life to save a stranger.

How could she deny feeling something for Mark when her stomach was too knotted up with fear for his safety to join Gerald in the kitchen for a cup of coffee?

Chapter Nine

An hour later, Mark took the steps to Amy's front porch two at a time. It might have been the longest hour of his life, knowing he couldn't leave his Lucky 13 crew or the woman he'd found in one of the back rooms of the burning house until the fire was contained and the scene was secure. Although it had been a relief to see Amy alive and well, he'd known a stab of jealousy at seeing Matt getting those few minutes of conversation with her by her truck.

He was the one who cared that she was all right. *He* was the one who'd had to remind himself more than once that Amy was tall, leggy and built like a curvy farm girl. So, even without being able to recognize the woman's face, he'd known the petite thing he'd carried out the front window behind Ray Jackson wasn't her. He should have felt guilty at feeling even one moment of respite that the badly burned woman the paramedics hadn't been able to revive wasn't Amy.

A woman was dead.

Another fire had consumed Amy Hall's property.

He'd finally had a chance to read the texts she'd sent him tonight. She'd been in trouble. Upset about something. She'd needed him.

And he hadn't been there for her. Not for any of it.

Mark draped his turnout coat over the porch railing and set his helmet on top, scratching his fingers through his hair since heat, sweat and a whole lot of water had plastered it to his head. He knocked on the door before checking the time on his utility watch, hoping it wasn't too late to pay a quick visit. He needed Amy in his arms. He needed to see her face up close and personal to know she was all right. He needed to tell her that he was ready to take whatever this was between them to the next level.

Hell, he was already at that level. He wouldn't be worrying and jealous and anxious to touch her if he wasn't feeling *next level* for her.

He held his breath when he heard the dead bolt disengage, then emptied his lungs on a deep sigh when he saw her.

Amy had changed into jeans and an aqua blue tank top that hugged every womanly curve. He did a quick check from head to toe, finding her face had been washed clean of makeup to reveal a pale canvas dotted with freckles. That silver knot pendant rested between her lush breasts, rising and falling with every breath. And she was barefoot. Her toenails were painted a shade of turquoise darker than her shirt.

And just as he acknowledged the hammer of desire that hit him at the sight of her naked, colorful toes, she grabbed one of his suspender straps and tugged him over the threshold. The foyer was dark. The door closed, and then he stumbled back against it when she pushed at his chest, stretched up on tiptoe and sealed her mouth against his.

The tension in Mark unfurled as Amy moved her soft lips over his. Then a whole different sort of tension grabbed hold. Mark settled one hand at her waist, pulling her hips closer to his. He tunneled his fingers into the thick waves of hair at her nape, cupping the back of her neck and tilting her head back a fraction to pull her full bottom lip between both of his and demand he be an equal partner in this unexpected kiss.

Amy's hands fisted in the front of his shirt, pinching the skin and muscle underneath and sending little electric shocks of heat through his body. She leaned into him and the kiss, and Mark was aware of every soft curve pillowing against his harder frame. He felt the cold metal of her pendant caught between them. He felt the heat of her lips and tongue, testing, tasting, parting, asking and answering every eager foray, every soothing touch, every needy claim of his own mouth on hers.

It might have been seconds, it might have been forever, before he heard the soft mewling sounds in her throat. Whether they were a reluctant protest or an unsatisfied hunger, Mark felt the frustrating flexing and pushing of her hands on his chest and broke off the kiss. Their ragged breaths blended as he rested his forehead against hers. Amy's green-gold eyes opened beneath his, looking up into his gaze with a frown of confusion, a bit of surprise and a dozen questions that probably matched his own gaze.

"Hello to you, too." His voice was a husky rasp from deep in his throat. "I should warn you, my boots are pretty messy—"

Amy silenced his teasing by pressing her finger to his lips. Then she touched the same finger to her own lips in the universal sign for quiet and grasped his hand to pull him into step behind her.

She pointed to the dimly lit living room off the foyer, and he saw her neighbor, the elderly black man—Sanders something—sleeping in the living room recliner. The older man who'd upset her the last time he'd seen her must be a welcome guest now because someone had covered him in a crocheted afghan. Or maybe because of the man's age, she didn't see him as any kind of threat.

Amy pointed out the low clearance of the scaffolding that arched across the foyer, and Mark ducked and willingly followed the pull of her hand to a first-floor bedroom where she peeked in on her sleeping grandmother before closing the door and leading him down the hallway into the kitchen. He squinted against the bright lights shining down from the ceiling, inhaled the sustaining smell of freshly brewed coffee and planted his feet, stopping Amy with a tug against her hand.

When she turned to face him, Mark buried his fingers in the silky thickness of her copper-red hair one more time, angling her mouth to reclaim it with his own. He backed her against the countertop, needing the anchor to brace them both as he drove his tongue inside her mouth to taste the sweet heat of her instant response.

He'd suspected her touch would be incendiary, that his body would react like tinder to a flame. But greeting him with a kiss that hinted at desperation and relief as much as it did bottled-up desire had ignited a different kind of fire in him. Yes, he wanted her. He wanted to pull off that tank top and set her up on this counter and find out exactly where this fiery chemistry would lead them.

But more than that, he wanted to understand if she truly felt the same connections their bodies did. Kissing Amy assuaged a lot of emotions that had been roiling inside him. But it also raised questions he needed answers to. He was falling for her. Falling harder and faster than he had for any other woman. Did that kiss—did this kiss—

mean the same thing to her that it did to him? Did she care? Did she want? Did she need him the way he needed her?

This time, Amy pulled away. Her uneven breathing warmed the skin above his collar as she rested her forehead at the juncture of his neck and shoulder. She wound her arms around his waist and snuggled in, cooling passion to comfort. Mark willingly wrapped his arms around her, breathing in the herbal scent of her hair and the faintest notes of sulfur and ozone that clung to her clothes and hair, no doubt from the welding work she did in her studio. He felt a little raw himself and craved the soothing warmth and softness of her body settling against his.

"Is the fire out?" Her whisper tickled the skin at the base of his throat.

Mark had to think about that for a second. She was talking about the structure at the bottom of the hill, not the sexual chemistry still simmering inside him. Distance. He needed distance and something cold to splash onto his skin to replace the fire she generated by clinging to him if he wanted to think straight. He tilted his face to the paneled ceiling and exhaled a heated breath before pressing a kiss to her temple. "It's contained enough that I could take off for a few minutes. It won't reignite and nothing else should collapse." He shifted his hands to the more neutral position of her shoulders but couldn't help stroking the soft skin of her arms as he pulled back. Her hair hung in loose waves around her face and he brushed a long tendril behind her ear before he resolutely moved away. He folded his arms across his chest, keeping his hands firmly tucked away from the impulse to touch her. "My brother said you wanted to see me."

"I didn't tell him that. I asked about you, but…" She crossed her arms beneath her breasts, matching his deceptively impersonal stance. "Why did you kiss me just now?"

Mark arched a questioning brow. Um, hadn't she started this kissing thing? Had he misread the whole *next level* connection between them tonight? But then he saw the tightness around her slightly swollen lips and read the doubt behind her bold question. For some reason, Amy wasn't used to following her impulses. Those two weeks of texting, sharing so much, yet keeping him at a distance, told Mark a lot about her willingness to trust. But who? Men? Him? Herself? What had happened in her past to make such a wildly creative and headstrong free spirit be so guarded with her personal life?

He suspected complete honesty was the only way to earn this woman's trust. He shrugged, attempting to take the anxious concern he'd felt out of his tone. "You're too pale. I remember how scared you were when we found your friend after that last fire. I know you must have seen me carrying that body out. Figured it would trigger some bad memories. I wanted to feel your energy, know that you're okay." He raked his fingers through his hair, admitting another truth. "I was jealous of my own damn brother because he had the chance to talk to you and I couldn't."

"You were in the middle of risking your life—of saving someone else's life. It was nice of your brother to check on me."

Right. Save a life? Apparently, that was a skill he'd lost somewhere along the way. But she didn't need to know what he'd found in that house. Not yet. So, he went with a joke. "You're talking about my taciturn big brother? You sure have a funny first impression of my family. First you think my dad is sexy, and now you think Matt is nice?"

"I must have been projecting some aura that told him I was worried." She reached up to smooth his hair across his forehead. It was a tender, intimate gesture, putting her fingers into his admittedly damp and messy hair. And yeah, it took a little of the edge off his concern for her. "I was scared when I realized it was you running out of that fire."

"So, you kissed me at the front door because you were scared?"

"I kissed you because…" She pulled her hands together in front of her, as if she needed to control the urge to touch him, as well. "I needed to know that you were okay, too."

When he realized she was shaking, Mark gave up on the idea of keeping his distance and pulled her into his arms. Her hands snaked around his waist to fist in the back of his T-shirt as he palmed her head and nestled her into that sweet spot where she fit so perfectly against his neck and shoulder. "Hey. It's okay. I'm fine. Just doin' my job, Red."

"I know, Fire Man. I know you're well trained, and you have your crew there to back you up. But you shouldn't have to come here, to *my* property, to fight fires that shouldn't be happening. You and your brother and everyone else shouldn't have to risk your life because some jerk is trying to hurt *me*." He could still feel the tremors ebbing from her body, but he got the idea from her words that her fear had transformed into anger, and it was now abating as she reassured herself that he was in one piece. They stood there, holding each other for several moments before Amy rubbed her nose against the column of his throat and breathed in deeply. Her smile felt like a soft kiss against his skin. "You smell like you've been fighting a fire."

"Sorry." Right. Smoke and sweat weren't big turn-ons. Mark started to pull away, but Amy pushed her body into his and held on tighter.

"Don't apologize. I'm just glad you're here. Like you said, you were doing your job. You smell like *you*." She eased her death grip on the back of his shirt and reached up to stroke her fingers along his jaw. "Like hard work and honesty. Strength and doing the right thing."

"Uh, none of those are scents, Red."

"Maybe that's what I feel from you." She pushed away from his chest, but her fingers lingered on his face. "Like art. It's not always an exact representation, but the feeling you get from the piece. I told you that you were a work of art."

Although her purposeful exploration of his features was a surprising turn-on, there was something about her smile that seemed forced. "Is this about more than the fire? You being scared? Did something happen tonight at your fancy party?" Her fingers stilled against his cheek, telling him something had. "I just had a chance to read your last text before running up here. It's a stupid nickname, but why do you need Captain Good Guy vibes? Are you okay?"

Amy pulled away entirely. She pulled out a chair from the table and invited him to sit. "Could I get you some coffee? It's decaf. Cold water? A beer?" Nice deflection of the question, but maybe she needed a few minutes to sort her thoughts and regain control of her emotions, too.

"I'm still on duty. But I'll take the water if it's cold." While Amy opened the fridge and brought a couple of bottles of water to the table, Mark washed up at the farmhouse sink. She was already sitting in a chair around the corner of the table from his when he joined her.

Amy watched him take a couple of long, cooling drinks before she spoke. "Derek Roland, Jocelyn's boyfriend, got drunk at the reception tonight. I tried to help him out. Watched him puke. Called him a car service. Argued at his office about stealing Jocelyn's research. Accused him of hurting her." She rolled her bottle between her hands on top of the table, drawing his attention to the purple marks on her wrist and hand. "This hasn't been a great night."

When Mark saw the fresh marks of brutality on her pale skin, he caught her hand and turned it gently, inspecting the severity of the bruises. There were five of them, almost fitting the span of his own hand. "Did he do this?"

"Like I said, he was drunk." She pulled away, perhaps sensing the anger simmering in him. She crossed her legs in her chair, sitting pretzel-style and self-contained, away from his touch, and reached for the open laptop on the table she must have been perusing before he knocked on her door. "Derek had her laptop all along. The police have been looking for it. I'm supposed to turn it in to Detective Beck in the morning."

Mark rested his elbows on his knees and leaned toward her, glancing from Amy to the icons on the computer screen and back to Amy. "What am

I missing here? Beck doesn't suspect you again, does she?"

Amy shook her head. She pulled her hair from behind her back and twisted it into a loose braid over her shoulder. He wondered if sitting still was ever an option for this woman. "I don't think so. But I may be the closest thing she has to a witness. I've done a cursory search through Joss's files, but they're mostly work related to her dissertation. Correspondence with her parents. A couple of applications for teaching positions at Cal Tech and Columbia University."

"She didn't want to stay in Kansas City?"

"She wants—wanted—to go where the interesting jobs are."

Mark pushed up straight again. "Did her boyfriend know she planned to leave?"

She considered that. Maybe Derek had an even stronger motive for killing Jocelyn than getting caught stealing her research. "I'll let Detective Beck know that's a possibility."

The same tension that had gripped him when he first realized Amy's bruises had been put there by a man's hand resurfaced. "Does Derek know you're reporting all this to the police?"

"I told him I was turning over the laptop."

His suspicion about the threat surrounding Amy grew even grimmer. "Did you have to wrestle it away from him?"

"No. I just took it off his desk. The argument happened afterward."

Mark wanted an explanation. There were too many crimes surrounding Amy and her fragile grandmother for him not to know the facts. She might not realize it yet, but it had become his personal mission to protect her from the things he'd seen two weeks ago and again tonight in that fire. "Give me details, Red. Why did Roland manhandle you? Why the hell are you doing KCPD's job?"

"Because I need answers. And I think I can find them faster than they can and make this all go away." Yeah, but at what cost? Putting herself in the literal line of the next fire? "Derek told me he was the last person to see Jocelyn alive. For a while there, I thought he'd done something to her. He was so distraught tonight."

"Could have been an act."

She finally opened her water and took a sip. "He confessed to stealing the laptop. But I don't think he hurt her."

Mark traced his fingers along the marks on her wrist. "He hurt *you*." It wasn't just his training that had him on his feet and opening her freezer. He found a bag of frozen peas in the door and carried them back to the table, where he placed them on her injuries to help the bruising and swelling reduce a little bit. It wasn't much, but it felt right to do something to ease her pain and give her some of the support she needed. He pulled his chair closer to face her straight on before he sat again. "Sounds like a reason for a serious argument. Could he be one of those possessive guys who thinks that if he can't have the woman he desires, then no one can?"

"Their relationship wasn't like that. At least, Joss never indicated there were any physical threats." She paused, and it took everything in him not to pull her into his arms and hold on until all this murder and arson mess had passed. "I should probably tell you…" She looked off into the shadows of the hallway beyond the kitchen. Ah, hell. Something was really wrong. It wasn't like the Amy Hall he knew to hesitate to share her thoughts.

"What?" He rested a hand on her knee, gently demanding her attention. "You can tell me anything, Red."

Her hazel eyes studied every nuance of his expression, determining the sincerity of that statement before she nodded. "I have PTSD. My argument with Derek triggered a bit of a panic attack. My first instinct after getting away was to get a hold of you."

"That's a good instinct to have."

"I don't want you to think I'm crazy or anything—"

"I'm not Dale O'Brien. You feel what you feel. You do what you need to do. That doesn't make you crazy." He squeezed her knee through her jeans. Then, with a legitimate excuse of checking her for other injuries, he tugged on her leg, and then the other, pulling her feet across his lap. He closed one hand around the arch of her foot and ran the other up to her thigh and back to her calf, gently massaging the tension he felt in her, or maybe just creating an outlet for the tension inside him. "Why do you have post-traumatic stress?"

If it had anything to do with this Derek Roland, he was going to punch the guy. But Amy sure as hell didn't need any more violence in her life. So, he forced himself to breathe deeply and kept rubbing her legs and feet as though he was soothing an injured animal.

She wiggled her toes in his grip and gave him a weary smile. "That feels fantastic. Those shoes I was wearing tonight about did me in."

"Red." He urged her to continue.

"Two years ago, my last boyfriend… It was a stupid Svengali thing that I shouldn't have fallen for now that I look back on it—"

"Amy." He needed her to focus, to spit it out before he lost the patience to handle whatever trauma she'd faced. And somehow, he knew she'd faced it on her own. That would never happen again. Not if he became part of her life the way he wanted to.

"When I discovered he was cheating, and I

broke it off, he assaulted me." The massage paused for a moment. Mark thought his jaw might crack because he was clenching it so hard at the thought of anyone putting cruel hands on this woman. But the battle to maintain an impassive expression was worth it when she went on. "Beat me up pretty good. Pushed me down a flight of stairs."

Mark swore, unable to remain impassive when he imagined her lush, pale body bruised and broken. "Please tell me you reported him."

He didn't realize his hands had stopped moving until Amy pulled away, hugging her knees to her chest. "He served time. I got him fired from his position at the university art department. He tried to blackmail me into not telling the police or the dean's office by keeping me from finishing my PhD. I filed charges against him from the hospital."

"He was a professor? One of *your* professors? He already had the power of grades and success over you, and then he…?"

"Preston had an artistic temperament."

Unable to go along with her attempt to lighten the conversation, Mark muttered a very choice word about what this Preston asswipe needed to have happen to him.

The tightness left Amy's expression, her eyes widened with surprise and she smiled at his curse. "What? Captain Good Guy knows some bad words, too."

Her smile widened, and some of the tension in him faded away. She dropped her feet to the floor and rested her hands atop the fists that he'd clenched on each knee of his bunker pants. "Preston Worth is old news. You don't need to rescue me from him. He doesn't even live in Missouri anymore. He's in Montana."

"What is your hang-up with rescuing you? I'm not okay with someone hurting you."

"Derek didn't really hurt me tonight." The bruises on her hand and wrist told another story, but he held his tongue. "But his office is at the top of a flight of stairs. Fighting with him reminded me of that last night with Preston." She squeezed her eyes shut and shook her head. "And so many men have hands. I don't like most of them."

"What?"

When she opened her eyes and tapped against his fists, he relaxed his hands and she laced her fingers with his. "I like yours, though."

"You don't always make sense," he confessed. But he liked the feel of her hands tangled with his. "I'm so sorry you had to go through that. No wonder you're gun-shy about getting involved with someone again."

"I'm not afraid of you, Fire Man. I don't think you'd ever hurt me." Her gaze dropped to the clasp of their hands on his knees, and he suspected that she truly believed that. "But what would you get out of getting involved with me?"

He considered that for a moment. Sure, there was the sexual pull he felt toward Amy. And as a Taylor, he'd been raised to serve and protect others long before his firefighter training had fine-tuned that calling. He wasn't naive enough to pretend that some of this need didn't have to do with redemption. He'd failed his grandfather, and he wasn't sure he could survive failing to help anyone else he cared about. That was one reason he'd been avoiding his own grandmother. "A few minutes of peace and quiet."

For his soul. For his conscience. For his future.

Amy's eyes widened. "Talk about not making sense. Peace and quiet? With me?" Without confessing his mistakes, it was easy for her to misinterpret his answer. "I'm not an easy relationship. I have opinions." He arched an eyebrow in a universal *Duh* expression and she grinned. "I have issues. A temper. Sometimes, I freak out. And, apparently, I have an enemy." Her breath puffed out in a sigh. "Or several."

"You think I can't handle all that?"

"You shouldn't have to."

"Isn't that my decision to make?" He reached out to sift the end of her braid through his fingers. "Unless you tell me to go, I'm going to be here for you. You reached out to me for a reason. And I don't think it's because I have an interesting face and likable hands. Whatever that means."

She caught his hand and linked their fingers

again. "You also give a hell of a foot massage, and you definitely know how to kiss."

He chuckled at the compliment and felt his cheeks warm. "I hadn't heard that one yet."

"You're adorable when you do that." She brushed her fingers across his heated skin. "In a manly man kind of a way. It humanizes you. Makes me think you need a little bit of protecting, too."

"And yet you still won't go out on a date with me."

She finally pulled away, tucking her legs up against her chest on the chair again, ignoring his joke. "Letting you rescue me makes me feel like a victim. And I don't want to feel that way ever again. Needing help—needing anyone—makes me feel like I'm dropping my guard or giving up. I'm strong because I've had to be. Gran needs me to be strong to take care of her, to take care of this place—to take care of myself so she doesn't worry herself into a heart event or stroke." He'd ask about Comfort Hall's health issues later, but he needed to hear the end of this story before Amy changed the subject to something less personal and painful. "Tonight, on campus, though, I couldn't seem to calm myself by doing any of the mantras or meditations my therapist taught me. I feel better, safer—centered—with you here. But I'm afraid that makes me weak."

"You don't think it takes a strong person to

admit that they could use a little help? That's smarts, not weakness."

"What about you, Mark? Do you ever ask for help?" Damn it if she wasn't turning the tables on him. "Like with whatever it is that makes you so sad? I catch glimpses of it. When you're not trying to make me laugh and you're not busy being Captain Good Guy and saving the day. Does your family help you with that? Or are you trying to be all strong on your own, too?"

Mark stood, paced to the kitchen archway and over to the sink, where he finished off the last of his water and searched for the recyclable bin near the back door to drop it inside. Hell. Should he admit he felt more centered being here with her, too? More normal than he'd felt in months? He'd been so worried, but touching her, holding her, talking to her—all seemed to ease that raw, self-doubting place inside him. She'd opened up to him, let him in. He'd dated other women, one for a lot longer than he'd known Amy, and he'd never felt as close to them as he did the copper-haired tomboy sitting across the room from him tonight.

He hadn't felt like he could share the guilt he felt over Grandpa Sid's death before. But Amy was so intuitive, so caring—so strong, despite her fears to the contrary—that he was tempted to be as honest with her as she'd been with him. But he couldn't. He wouldn't dump that on her, too. Although he wasn't quite clear on the distinction between helping her and rescuing her that she took such issue with, he was damn clear on the idea that *he* wasn't the one who needed to be rescued tonight.

"Struck a nerve, huh?" He could hear her getting up behind him, closing the laptop, straightening chairs. "It's not so easy, is it? Baring your soul to someone? Trusting them with your inner truths? Admitting you can't handle everything on your own?" An edge of sarcasm entered her tone. "I still don't see what you'd get out of this relationship if you won't talk to me. Seems pretty one-sided to me."

"One problem at a time. Okay, Red?" He leaned his hips against the sink and faced her, holding on to the edge of the counter on either side of him. She stuffed the peas in the freezer door and closed it, waiting for him to continue. "I'm not ready to talk about it yet," he admitted.

"But you will talk about it with somebody?" she pushed. "If not me, then a friend or family member? A therapist?"

Mark nodded. "I will. But tonight, we deal with the fire and figuring out who set it."

"And keeping me safe." The sarcasm left her tone and she smiled. "So you can get those few minutes of peace and quiet."

Some of the tension in him eased at her understanding. "Keeping you safe is a given." He pushed away from the counter to capture her injured hand and folded it gently into his own. "My team will be here awhile, checking for hot spots, rolling up hoses and cleaning up the debris."

"Aren't you supposed to help with that, too?"

"They can manage without me for a few minutes longer." Since she seemed to be willing to let him touch her, Mark wasn't inclined to let go. "Will you walk with me?"

They headed through the darkened house and back onto the porch. The lights from the fire trucks pointed toward the charred shell of the smoldering structure, leaving the ground between them and the house in darkness. With the omnipresent construction scaffolding casting more shadows than illumination from the porch light, the late summer night swallowed them up like a blanket.

When Mark paused at the railing to watch his crew checking for any embers that could reignite and structural issues that could collapse on the firefighters or the investigators who would be here soon, Amy leaned against his arm, resting her cheek on his shoulder.

"It's another arson fire, isn't it?" She sounded more resigned than surprised.

Mark nodded. "Looks that way. There were pour marks from an accelerant on the mattress."

"At least O'Brien can't accuse me of setting this one. I have over a hundred witnesses who saw me on the WU campus tonight."

"He's more of a suspect than you are." He pointed to the housing development across the lake. O'Brien's trailer was still lit up, and the beat-up car of a couple of his workers was still parked beside his white truck. "He and all the men who work for him were here when we arrived. A bunch of lookie-loos. Not one of them drove over here to check on your grandmother."

"Great neighbors, huh? Thank God for Mr. Sanders. He's not the friendliest tenant, but he does seem to care about Gran. He alerted her to the fire."

"Amy…" Mark turned and sat on the railing, pulling her between his legs, to keep her close and their conversation hushed, as though his words might carry to the men across the lake. "I know you saw me carry a body out of the house—"

He thought he detected a shiver. "Can you tell me who it was? Our tenants who lived there moved out almost two months ago. Did we have a squatter? A homeless guy?"

He settled his hands at her waist, offering the support he suspected she'd need. "It was another woman. Her skull was crushed, and she was set on fire."

"Just like Jocelyn." Definitely a shiver. He slipped his fingertips beneath the hem of her tank top and felt the chill on her skin. But her hands were braced against his biceps, keeping him from drawing her closer. "Do you know who she is?"

"We got to the fire sooner this time," he explained. "The body wasn't completely incinerated, but I suspect she was dead from her injuries or smoke inhalation before we ever got to her. There was a purse with her. The plastic in her wallet hadn't melted yet, so there was a name. Autopsy will have to confirm it's her purse, but it looks like Dale O'Brien's assistant."

"Lissette Peterson?"

"You knew her?"

"Not well. We met once when I went in to argue with O'Brien. She was nice. Polite, when she probably didn't have to be."

"The woman had to be a saint to work for him."

Amy nodded, but her gaze moved beyond him to the lake. "The men who work for O'Brien were all there tonight, waiting for paychecks because he didn't know how to do the books and handle payroll. I'm sure Lissette did that for him."

"Sounds like she's been missing for some time if that wasn't taken care of." Mark released her long enough to pull out his phone. "I'll call my brother Pike at KCPD, see if she was reported missing. I'll have him check to see that your old boyfriend— What was his name?"

"Preston Worth."

"I want to make sure he's still in Montana and nowhere near you."

Amy hugged her arms around her waist and listened in while Mark made the call. Pike promised answers by morning, if not sooner. By the time he hung up, Amy was perched on the railing beside him. "I doubt if Derek ever met Lissette. You might convince me he had a motive to kill Jocelyn, but he'd have no reason to go after Lissette."

"Unless tonight was a diversion, meant to cover up his original crime and make KCPD think they have a serial killer on their hands."

"That's an unsettling thought. Poor Lissette." She shrugged. "But Derek was at the same reception I was all evening."

"Did you have eyes on him all night?"

"Well, no. I saw him before the dinner, but I didn't really talk to him until after the speeches. He was outside when I was ready to leave. I stayed longer to try to sober him up."

"How long does it take to get here from Williams U and back? Forty minutes? An hour if there's traffic?" He reached for her hand, lacing their fingers together again. "You need to share that possibility with Detective Beck, too."

"He would have had to have been acting drunk to pull that off." He saw the exact moment in her upturned expression when she realized that Roland could pull off something like that. Uncomfortable with the possibility of a friend's betrayal or his touch, Amy hopped down and started to pace. "His emotions were way over-the-top tonight. I thought it was grief."

"He could have been responsible even if he didn't leave your party." Her face was alternately dappled by bright light and shadows as she moved across the porch, making it difficult to tell if she was angry or afraid. "Fires can be set by a delayed ignition, too. You said he's a science guy, right? Anyone with basic chemistry or electrical experience could rig something like that."

She stopped in front of him with a mix of emotions crossing her face. Mostly anger, he'd say. "Are you trying to reassure me or scare me to death?"

"I'm being real with you. I don't want you to ever think that I'm not telling you the truth."

"I appreciate that." She tapped her fist against his thigh, then drummed it faster and faster until she threw her arms out in a burst of frustration. "Who is setting these fires? Is Derek covering up his crimes? Did Jocelyn and Lissette stumble across someone like O'Brien burning down buildings on our property, and this guy is silencing his witnesses?" Her temper ebbed, and the gruesomeness of what she was thinking seeped into her voice. Her fingers remained on his thigh, squeezing, kneading, clinging to him even if she didn't fully realize it. "Or are *they* the crime, and the fires are the cover-up? Is any woman in this part of the city safe? Are Gran and I safe?"

"Exactly." Mark covered her hand with his to still the pulsing movement and pulled her to him again.

"I need to know why someone is trying to burn you out of house and home." He hunched his shoulders slightly, so he could look straight into those beautiful green-gold eyes. "And why I shouldn't be afraid that you're next on this guy's list."

Chapter Ten

Amy pushed her face mask up on top of her welding helmet and stood back to admire her work. Instead of celebrating that she was nearing completion on her latest metals project, she frowned. "Needs more color."

This garden alien was supposed to be a fun piece, a cartoonish figure meant to add height to her client's backyard garden. But instead of building a whimsical sculpture that reflected the young family's playful style, she'd ended up with a stark, metallic *Doctor Who* villain that looked like it had just rolled off an industrialized war machine assembly line.

She shook her head at the copper robot. "That'll scare the kids."

Heck. It scared her. Setting her helmet aside and hanging her welding torch over its hook, she glanced around her studio. For a piece this size, she needed something bigger than the broken bits of glass and rocks on her shelves. The purple crystal geode sitting on her workbench would work for the creature's nose. But she wanted a pair of colored glass bottles to add as drop earrings, or maybe she could find some old fencing to extend as antennae on top of the figure. Some colorful beer and pop bottle caps could be grouped together to make eyes and blushing cheeks.

Now that the creative juices had kicked in, Amy was thinking more positively. She pulled up the sleeve of her blue coveralls past the deep purple bruises that had worried Mark so last night and checked her watch. Sleep had been elusive after Mark and his crew from Firehouse 13 had driven away, taking all their lights and activity and reassuring company with them. After checking in on Gran and Mr. Sanders, Amy had settled in upstairs to wrestle with nightmares about crashing down stairwells and being swallowed up by flames. And then her waking mind had raced with memories and future possibilities, both good and bad, as she sorted out her unexpected feelings for Mark. Once she'd decided how easy and risky it would be to not only depend on him, but to fall in love with him, she'd gotten up early to lose herself in her art studio.

But she lacked the materials her imagination wanted her to use, and with her 9:00 a.m. appointment with Detectives Beck and Carson at Fourth Precinct headquarters, the clock was ticking. She should set the sculpture aside, put away her gear and take a quick walk to clear her head before Mark came by the house to pick her up.

Between pulling Mark into the house to kiss the stuffing out of him and sitting out on the porch and kissing him good-night, something had changed in Amy. Her resolve had shifted. She'd admitted her fears and shortcomings. She'd surrendered some of her independence and strength by needing Mark so desperately last night. She'd made herself vulnerable by sharing her past mistakes. But maybe she'd gained something, as well. She was strong enough to admit that she was out of her league with murderers and arsonists, that she stood a better chance of finding justice for Jocelyn and possibly saving other lives if she accepted Mark's help.

And, perhaps more important, she'd discovered that her heart had healed enough to let someone new into her life.

She was strong enough to risk falling in love again.

As Amy slipped off her coveralls and buttoned a cotton blouse over her tank top and jeans, she replayed how last night had ended.

"I'LL GO WITH you to see Detective Beck in the morning," Mark offered. His tone was casual, like he was making plans to meet a friend for coffee. But his calloused fingertips, tickling the

skin at her waist and back beneath the hem of her top, told a different story. They clenched and released, as though reluctant to let her go. As though Mark didn't want to let her out of his sight, not even for a moment.

"That isn't necessary," she assured him. She knew the way to the precinct. She'd call a friend to come stay with Gran, or maybe see if Gerald had plans for the day. If their neighbor was good to her grandmother, then Amy could put up with his grumpy personality.

"Not negotiable, Red. Unless I'm out on a call, I'll be here to pick you up. And if I'm still out with my crew, I'll send one of my brothers. You're not doing any more of this on your own."

"Do you know how much I'm bristling at you giving me orders like that?"

His hands tightened on her hips, pulled her closer. "Do you know how much I need you to be safe? How much it kills me to know that you don't feel safe in your own home? On your own land?"

Amy reached up to stroke her fingertips across the taut angles of his cheek and jaw. She brushed her fingers across his stubbled skin, once, twice, again, until she felt the tension in his expression ease.

And then he palmed the back of her head and covered her mouth with his. Her lips parted on a soft gasp of pleasure and he thrust his tongue inside, staking a claim she willingly surrendered. Amy circled her arms around his neck and pulled *her body flush against his hardness and heat. A fire ignited inside her, heavy and molten, shooting sparks to the tips of her breasts where they rubbed against his chest and pooling between her thighs as she felt his response swelling against her belly.*

Whistles and catcalls from the bottom of the hill, and the blast of one loud engine horn startled Amy from the madness that had consumed her.

"Mark." She flattened her hands on his broad shoulders and pushed some space between them. "We have an audience."

Even through the murky light seeping through the porch scaffolding, she could see the blush on his cheekbones. Amy had no doubt her face was just as red. Instead of moving apart, he turned his hands to squeeze her bottom and pulled her in to reclaim her lips. "They're jealous."

But despite the wanton urge to crawl right onto his lap, Amy pushed back, not wanting to give his coworkers any reason to make more noise that might wake her grandmother or Mr. Sanders. "Won't they give you grief for this public display of affection? Especially when you're supposed to be working right now?"

"Kiss me like that again and I won't care how much they tease me."

She laughed and slipped her fingers between their mouths when he tried to kiss her again. "I'm just looking out for your best interests, Fire Man. You'd better get back to work."

He pressed a ticklish kiss to her palm and eased his grip on her backside. "I'd better."

Amy moved away, surprised at how cool the air felt on her skin after being pressed so close to him. She handed him his coat and helmet. "Be safe. I'll see you in the morning."

Mark stood and set his helmet on top of his beautiful, mussed hair. "It's a date."

Amy followed him to the edge of the porch, hugging one of the posts as he jogged down the steps. "Driving me to the police station is not a date."

He faced her but continued backing his way down the hill to rejoin his crew. "If I bring you coffee or buy you lunch, it will be."

"Taylor!" the fire captain in the white helmet yelled. "Get your butt down here. I need a report."

"On my way, Cap!" he shouted over his shoulder. But he pointed to her. "You're going to go out with me yet."

"Taylor!"

"You'd better go."

"You're not alone, Red. Remember that." With that promise, Mark turned and jogged down the hill to speak to his captain. His brother Matt joined them. A minute later, their father, Gideon Taylor, climbed out of his KCFD SUV and strode over to the group.

No. With a family like that, Mark probably had no real idea of what it meant to be truly alone.

Alone was when the man you loved made no apologies for sleeping with other women, telling her she wasn't enough to make him happy.

Alone was when standing up for yourself was rewarded with a punch in the face and a shove down the stairs.

Alone was testifying against the bastard who'd beaten you and then tried to cover up his crime with blackmail that had silenced other victims.

Alone was knowing your best friend was missing and if you gave up the search, no one would find her.

Alone was protecting the woman who'd raised her from greedy contractors and dangerous fires and a sick threat that seemed to be closing in around her beloved home because there was no one else to do it.

How could she make Mark Taylor understand that she'd forgotten how to be part of a couple? How to trust implicitly that backup would be there when she needed it? How patient could he be with her while she relearned how to love? How much trouble was he willing to endure being involved with her?

How much was this going to hurt if she listened to her heart and Mark wound up getting injured because of her? How much was this going to hurt if he wised up and decided that a relationship with Crazy Amy Hall wasn't worth the risk?

Because she was tired of feeling alone. Of fighting alone.

She was ready to risk her heart on Mark Taylor. But was he ready to risk his heart on her?

With that philosophical debate weighing heavily on her heart and mind, Amy grabbed her backpack, where she carried Jocelyn's laptop, and fastened the padlock on the art studio door behind her.

Since she had time, she detoured through the surviving part of the old stables, finding a wooden tray of old skeleton keys and lock plates in the tack room that might work for her sculpture's earrings. There was no electricity in the damaged building, but with the morning sun shining through the collapsed roof and broken windows, she didn't need man-made light. Her exploration uncovered a rusted metal trowel that could be polished up and used as the creature's antenna if she could find another similar old tool somewhere on the property. Perhaps she could remove the peeling paint from the handle and repaint it a bright, vibrant color. She dusted off the items as best she could, then unzipped the front compartment on her backpack and tucked them inside. Joy bubbled up at her discovered treasures, and the idea for a humorous, more child-friendly garden alien became a finished piece in her mind.

But the image died, and the joy quickly dissipated as she turned and faced the back end of the stables. Still marked off by crisscrossing yellow tape, the charred timbers and chunks of roof piled inside and atop the old horse stalls were a stark reminder of the downward spiral her life had taken after Preston. Curious to know if she could truly put her past behind her, she walked closer, reaching over the restrictive tape to shove aside a broken door and pick up the burned frame of one of her canvases. The ruined pinewood crumbled into dust the moment she lifted it off the ground. She'd set all of her paintings she'd done under Preston's tutelage aflame that cathartic night when the first fire had gotten out of hand and she'd been forced to call 9-1-1. She'd burned the portrait Preston had painted of her. Even though the image had once made her feel beautiful, the way he'd treated her had not.

Amy shoved the old door back into the debris and brushed off her hands. Nope. Not even one flicker of regret or sorrow for the destroyed life she'd left behind. She'd proved herself stronger than her past. Tipping her chin up, she marched out of the stable, pausing at the spigot on the back of the house to wash her hands.

She was ready for her future. Ready to solve a murder. Ready to love again. She wound her fist around the knotted heart pendant hanging from her neck and smiled. She only hoped Mark Taylor was ready for her.

Amy had every intention of going back inside to wait for Mark, but when she rounded the house and saw the blackened walls and broken windows of the rental property that had burned last night, a glimmer of movement caught her eye. She paused at the railing leading up the steps and waited to see if what she'd seen had simply been a trick of the morning sunlight and her own movement.

There. Amy's grip tightened around the straps of her backpack. There was a light on inside the abandoned house. A house that had no electricity. Not since KCFD had shut off both the electrical and propane feeds last night.

Since there was no vehicle parked on the concrete pad in front of the house, Amy scanned both sides of the lake, looking for some clue as to what was going on. A looter? Curiosity-seeker? A light blazed through the windows of Gerald Sanders's living room, indicating he'd returned home and was reading his newspaper over coffee and breakfast. On the far side of the lake, she spotted Dale O'Brien's work truck in front of his office trailer. But there were no other vehicles there. No men reporting for work yet. Had O'Brien come in early? Or stayed the night? And why? Straightening up the mess of paperwork created by Lissette's absence? Or something more sinister? The man always seemed to show up when she least wanted to see him.

The light in the burned house flickered, drawing Amy's attention again. But it disappeared almost as quickly as she'd seen it. When it reappeared a few seconds later, passing by the shattered front window, curiosity and a familiar sense of anger and violation moved Amy's feet. Why the hell was the Hall farm such a target for criminals?

Someone was in that house, moving through it with a flashlight. She headed straight down the hill and crossed the asphalt. Her heart beat faster as she realized whoever was in there was looking for something. An intruder searching for treasures like she'd just found in the wreckage of the stables? An arsonist revisiting the scene of his crime, either reliving the adrenaline rush of his handiwork or retrieving something he'd inadvertently left behind?

The yellow warning tape crossing the front door and broken window hadn't stopped the trespasser from entering.

It wouldn't stop her, either. Amy pulled her cell phone from the side pocket of her backpack and pressed 9-1-1, holding her thumb above the Send key as she pushed open the front door. She couldn't go far before a collapsed wall and the skeletons of charred furniture forced her to step into what used to be the living room. "Hello?"

she called out to the intruder. "You shouldn't be here. Both for legal reasons and your own safety." She heard the screech of something heavy moving across the floor from the back of the house, followed by the scuffling of footsteps. "I have the police on speed dial. I'm calling them right now if you don't leave."

"Don't do that. Please." The next thing she knew, a bright light was shining in her face, blinding her. "You shouldn't be here, Miss Amy."

She exhaled the breath she'd been holding when she recognized Richie Sterling's voice. "Richie?"

When he saw her holding her hand in front of her face, he lowered the beam of his flashlight. "Sorry about that."

"You shouldn't be here, either." She showed him that she was clearing the number off her phone and tucked her cell into the pocket of her jeans. "My family's name is on the deed to this place."

"Huh?"

"I have the right to be here. You don't." Blackened carpet, still soaked from last night's fire hoses, stretched between them. This had once been the furnished living room, and though most of the furniture here was still in one piece, it had been ruined by smoke and water. Her steps squished as she crossed the room, heading toward the back of the house, where the hottest point of the fire had peeled wallpaper, warped floorboards and linoleum, and taken down interior walls and roof braces. She stopped in front of Richie, nodding toward the kitchen and bedroom at the back of the house. "What are you looking for?"

He shrugged. "I'm not looking for anything."

"Then why are you here?" She moved around him into what used to be the kitchen. The appliances were black with soot, and the countertops had melted, but the surviving cabinets had been opened. She didn't know enough about fighting fires to tell if that had happened during the fire or after. The air here was stale with the scents of sulfur and dampness, leftovers from the blaze and its aftermath. "Are you looking for copper piping?"

"Like you use to make your funny creatures."

Amy nodded. She doubted she had a competing artist here. It wouldn't be the first time someone had broken into one of the empty buildings over the years to steal metals that could be sold on the illegal market. "I know the copper is worth some money, but you can't take anything from here, Richie. The police and fire department are conducting an investigation. You might be disturbing evidence."

She startled at the touch of Richie's hand closing around her upper arm. "You shouldn't be here, Miss Amy." He parroted his greeting from earlier. His cheeks were redder than usual as he slid his hand down to hers and tugged. "I'll walk you out."

While his tone wasn't threatening and his grip wasn't painful, Amy had suffered too many recent encounters to be comfortable with him touching her. She pulled her hand away and smiled. "That's okay, Richie. I'd better check to make sure everything's secure before I leave."

"You have to go." He reached for her again, and Amy retreated a step. He ducked his head, his gaze darting back and forth across the floor. His voice came out on a whispered croak. "It's not safe."

It certainly didn't feel safe with a warning like that. "Richie, do you know something about what happened to Ms. Peterson? Or who's setting these fires?"

"There you are." Brad Frick's surly interruption sent Richie skittering several feet away from Amy. He strode from the front door to the kitchen, not caring what mess his work boots stepped in or tracked onto the ruined linoleum. Like a parent speaking to a naughty toddler, Brad snapped his fingers and pointed at Richie. "I told you to stay out of this place." He pulled off his paint-stained ball cap and nodded to Amy. "Sorry, Miss Amy. Richie's just curious about what burned-up places look like. He likes watching fires. Thinks they're cool."

Richie's downturned face finally lifted, and

he laughed. "Fires are cool. That doesn't make sense. Fires are hot."

"Get on out of there." Brad jerked his head toward the front door, ordering Richie to leave. As his lighter-haired partner shuffled past him, Brad's gaze darted toward the framed remains of the hallway and bedrooms beyond. Was he taking in the blackened scorch marks on the floor and standing timbers? Did he think watching something burn was cool, too? Had one of them set this fire? Set all the others?

Amy couldn't help but retreat another step as suspicion hammered through her pulse.

"You didn't take anything, did you, Richie?" Brad asked, his gaze coming back to Amy after he looked over his shoulder to his friend.

Richie frowned. "I didn't take anything. I didn't find it."

Find *it*? Find what? Had Richie been in here looking for something specific? Did Brad know what *it* was?

Before she could ask a question, Brad covered his receding hairline with his cap again and shooed Richie on out the door. "Come on. We'd better get over to O'Brien's and get to work." Once Richie was outside, he stopped at the door and glanced back at her. "Don't pay him no mind, Miss Amy. He's like a kid in the head. He don't mean nothing by what he says. You'd better leave, too. You wouldn't want to get in trouble with the police."

With that dubious warning, he left. A few seconds later, she heard the slam of two car doors at the back of the house and an engine turning over. With parts of the house damaged and missing, it was easy to see Brad's old blue car bouncing up onto the asphalt road and driving away.

Why had they parked behind the house in the dead grass? So they couldn't be spotted from the house? There didn't seem to be any good reason for hiding. Had Richie's slip of the tongue been something important? Had he broken in to look for something specific? Brad had known he was here. Had he sent Richie in to find something for him? Or had he been indulging his friend's dangerous fascination with fire?

There were so many things wrong with this encounter that Amy wanted answers before she went to talk to Detectives Beck and Carson. At the worst, Richie or Brad was hiding something. At the very least, they'd sneaked into a crime scene and had possibly disturbed evidence the detectives or Mark's dad would want to know about.

And since Brad's attention had been focused on the back bedrooms, and that was where Richie had come from, Amy crossed through the kitchen and walked into first one bedroom and then the next. The first had been burned from floor to ceiling, and there was a hole in the roof above her. But the second bedroom, the one where Lissette had been found, was in a whole other state of destruction.

Piles of ash littered the floor where wood furniture had stood. And the double mattress, cordoned off by more yellow tape, rested at a wonky angle beneath the missing back window. Had KCFD broken that window? Had the fire blasted it out of its frame? Or had the arsonist—and Lissette's killer—broken in that way? The wood slats beneath the mattress and box springs and plastic wheels on each leg of the bed were gone, leaving the metal frame supporting the hollowed-out mattress where Lissette must have spent her last moments.

Amy's coffee and breakfast bar curdled in her stomach. She didn't have to be an arson investigator to recognize the dark black pattern zigzagging across the mattress and pooling at the center where accelerant had been poured to hide the body. Although every surface in this room was stained by smoke and soot, more pour patterns circled the floor around the bed.

Moving closer, Amy remembered the absolute destruction of Jocelyn's remains, and her hand automatically went to the pendant on her chest, feeling the bond that had once linked them. Would she find anything similar here where Lissette had died? A piece of heirloom jewelry? The purse that Mark said had survived the conflagration? Had

Lissette Peterson been burned out of existence without any symbol of a good friend or loved one to cling to?

If there was anything here for Richie or Brad or anyone else to find, she didn't see it. No matches. No melted gasoline can. No lighter like the one she used to ignite her welding torch.

Creepy though he might be, Brad was right about one thing. She didn't need to be here, either.

Amy turned to step away, to respect the dead and the crime scene, when her foot crashed through one of the charred, warped floorboards. "Ow!" She tweaked her ankle as her work boot glanced off something metallic and wedged her leg in up to her knee. "What the hell?"

A couple of tugs only scraped her skin inside her jeans. The twinge in her ankle receded as her curiosity kicked in. Giving up on keeping her clothes clean, she sat down on the floor and turned on the flashlight of her cell phone. She shrugged off her backpack and shone her light down into the gap between the floor joists. The metal wasn't part of the house's construction. It was a box—a square metal strongbox that had been hidden beneath the floor. Had that been put there by an earlier resident? Amy glanced up at the door frame. Was this what Richie had been looking for?

Would he and Brad come back for it the mo-

ment she left? Provided she could get herself out
of here.

Amy pulled her phone back to call the police,
but she'd be going to the police station in a little while anyway, so she could mention it then.
Dale O'Brien certainly hadn't helped her reputation with the authorities any by pointing out
that she, too, had set a fire. What if this box had
nothing to do with Lissette's death and the fires?
Maybe she'd uncovered one of the former tenants' stash of porn or pot. No, she'd make sure
she had something significant here first, before
she gave Detectives Beck and Carson any more
reason to question her reliability as a witness or
even a suspect in their investigation.

Instead of calling the police, she texted Mark.
Running a little late. I got caught at the rental
house where the fire was last night. "Caught." She
shook her head, grinning wryly at the literalness
of her choice of words, before finishing and sending the text. My two handymen were checking the
place out. I had to shoo them away.

Then she snapped a picture of the hole in the
floor, the box and her boot. It didn't take her creative mind long to figure out a plan of escape.
She dug the old trowel out of her backpack and
wedged it between the floorboards, prying one
loose on either side of her leg. They came up
more easily than she'd expected because this section of flooring wasn't nailed down. Nails didn't

burn. So, these boards had been loose before the fire. Before Lissette's murder. Someone had made themselves a secure hiding place for whatever treasures were inside that box.

With more wiggle room now to move, Amy reached into the hidey-hole and untied her boot. Pulling her foot out released the tension that had trapped her and allowed her to twist her boot onto its side and pull it and the strongbox up. She scooted away to a sturdier stretch of charcoal floor to examine the metal box. It, too, had been blackened by the fire, but not destroyed. Scrubbing away the soot with the butt of her palm, she uncovered the familiar O'Brien Construction logo.

"What have you done now, Dale?" she murmured. Maybe he'd paid Brad and Richie to come here to find his stash of buried treasure. She took another picture before sinking back onto her heels and pulling the box onto her lap. The simple lock was no match for the trowel blade and she quickly pried it open. "What the…?"

Inside the box was a cigarette lighter. She also found a half-empty jar of petroleum jelly that had cotton balls stuffed inside. Her grandfather had once taught her that trick on a camping trip— petroleum jelly burned, even in rainy weather, providing enough tinder with the cotton to ignite a fire for thirty seconds or so. Enough to burn until kindling could be added to build the blaze. Were they enough to set an entire building on fire? Maybe if another accelerant was added to the mix.

But even those simple tools for starting a fire weren't what made the bile rise in her throat.

There were other items inside, yellowed with smoke damage and frayed at the corners, but she had no trouble identifying a stack of photographs printed out on cheap card stock. She took one more picture before tucking her phone into her jeans and lifting the pictures from the box. "Oh, my God. Oh. Oh." She felt like she might truly be sick as she sorted through the tainted photos. If these were Dale O'Brien's, the man had some serious issues. They weren't images of architectural works the contractor had built. They weren't pictures of fun-loving get-togethers or even scenery from a family vacation.

They were pictures of women.

A lot of women. All taken from a distance. All snapped without any of the women knowing.

Pictures of Jocelyn Brunt and Lissette Peterson.

Pictures of her.

Chapter Eleven

Amy's phone vibrated in her pocket, but she couldn't look away from the haunting images to answer the text.

Her hand shook as she identified the familiar scenes of Jocelyn in her Jeep, driving through the hills on the north end of the farm. Jocelyn bent over equipment, analyzing a soil sample and entering the data onto her laptop. Lissette Peterson coming out of the construction office. Sharing a conversation with a group of workers on the Copper Lake site, smiling.

There were images of Amy, hiking alongside the fence that bordered the old orchard, gathering discarded items from the nearby highway that she could use in her sculptures. Another picture of her standing on the front porch, leaning away from the scaffolding and turning her face to the warmth of the sunset.

There were other women she didn't know. Standing on the corner of a crosswalk in the city.

Walking across a parking lot at a shopping mall. There was a dark-haired woman sitting at a desk in an office somewhere, as though the picture had been covertly taken across a waiting room. None of the pictures were lewd. But they were all…invasive.

Her phone buzzed again, and she absently took it out of her pocket. Mark.

Get back to the house. On my way.

He understood the threat. All those times she'd felt as though she was being watched, she had been.

These women had been spied on. *She* had been spied on. Now at least two of those women were dead.

Were there other bodies out there? Would there be more bodies in the future?

Amy couldn't quite seem to catch a deep breath.

Would one of those bodies be hers?

"Frick! Sterling!" The sharp male voice shouting from the front of the house startled her from the terrible portents of her imagination.

She typed a quick text to Mark. Only one word. Hurry.

At the sound of approaching footsteps, Amy moved as fast as she could. She shoved her phone into her pocket. She stuffed the photos she held into her backpack, along with the trowel. She closed the lockbox and grabbed her boot and backpack. But she couldn't handle all of them at once. She couldn't handle any of them like this. Dropping her boot, she opened the main compartment of her backpack and tried to stuff the box inside, to keep searching or spying eyes from knowing she'd found it. But the box was too big, and the footsteps were too close. She unzipped the expanding feature on her pack, but with the laptop and her own things inside, there still wasn't enough room. She shoved the box into the top as best she could before slipping the straps around her arms and pushing to her feet.

"I thought I told you to meet me at..."

Amy spun around at the voice from the doorway. The box tilted in the top of her open pack and she squeezed her shoulders back, trying to keep it hidden from view. Her breath gusted through her nose as she tried to appear composed, unassuming, not worried one whit about Dale O'Brien standing there, snorting a laugh at her expense.

"Crazy Amy." He propped his hands at his bulky waist and stepped into the room, eyeing her from head to toe. "One shoe off and one shoe on. Nothing weird about that. At the scene of another fire. If the police ask, I'll have to tell them I found you here."

"I'll have to tell them you were here, too," she

countered, sounding bolder than she felt. "Why are you looking for Brad and Richie? Why did you think they'd be here—on my property?"

"I saw Brad's car parked behind the place. Thought I'd come over and chase them back to work." He swiped his finger along the charred frame of the door, studied the soot that came off and then pulled out a white handkerchief to wipe off his skin. "Some of my men are less inclined to come early or stay late with this rash of fires."

"And murders."

"And murders." He walked over to the bed. Amy picked up her boot and scuttled away, keeping more than an arm's reach between them. "I hear this is where your boyfriend found Lissette. Shame to die like that. She meant somethin' to me. She was a good employee. And she was... sweet. My men all liked her."

She thought of the pictures in her bag. Someone had liked her a lot. "Lissette was friendly to me."

"She would be." O'Brien studied the burn marks around the mattress, breathing in deeply, before he pulled off his hard hat and wiped the sweat from his forehead and cheeks with the soiled handkerchief. Or was he dabbing at tears? Could he be remembering Lissette's last moments? Or was he truly grieving for a friend? "Always friendly, that girl. Always sticking up for the underdog."

Amy's phone buzzed in her pocket again, but she didn't want to take her eyes off O'Brien as she drifted half a step toward the door. "You and Lissette were close?"

"You mean, was I boinking her?" He plopped the hard hat back on his head, his crass response erasing even that small bit of compassion she'd thought about feeling for him. "Nah. Wasn't for lack of trying. She said I was too old for her." Amy kept inching toward the door but found him circling the bed to keep the distance between them from increasing. In fact, whether it was intentional or not, he was moving her toward the back wall now, away from the exit, unless she wanted to try to muscle her way past him. Muscling hadn't worked against Preston Worth. It hadn't worked against Derek Roland. She doubted it would work against a man O'Brien's size, either. "Besides, she had a strictly hands-off policy with the men she worked with. Most of them respected that."

"Most of them? Who didn't?" Was climbing onto the mattress and diving out that window an option? It couldn't be that far to the ground outside a single-story house. As long as the mattress didn't collapse beneath her. And she could move faster than the overweight man. Amy shifted closer. "Did you respect her wishes?"

Instead of getting an answer to her probing questions, the metal box chose that moment to shift out of her bag. Her scrambling efforts to catch it before it hit the floor only rattled the contents and pushed it away from her. It tumbled to a stop at O'Brien's feet.

"What do you have here?" He picked it up before she could snatch it away from him. "This looks like one of mine." He turned it over to inspect where she'd rubbed the soot off the remnants of the O'Brien Construction Company logo. "You stealing from me?"

She should have been moving toward the window, not trying to retrieve the box. Because now she was close enough to smell O'Brien's coffee breath and stale sweat. And there was no mistaking that he meant to corner her in this room.

"You're kidding, right?" Amy sassed, as though fear wasn't pounding through her veins. If that box was his, then that fire-starting kit and those pictures must be his sick obsession, too. She stepped back toward the window.

But suddenly he was right in front of her. The backs of her knees bumped against the mattress. "I've had a couple of them go missing over the past few weeks."

"First you accuse me of arson, and now you accuse me of stealing?" Amy pulled up to her full height, even though she was shaking inside. "Are you sure you want to claim that box? I found it hidden under those floorboards. I think Richie might have been looking for it." She pointed to the hole in the floor, hoping he'd at least turn, if not move, toward it. But the big blob didn't budge. Amy tilted her chin. "Question is, was he searching on his own accord? Or was he doing a job for you? Is that why you wanted them to meet you early this morning?"

He tucked the box under his arm. "My property, my business."

"So, you admit you know what's inside," she accused.

"You have been nothing but trouble from the first time I met you. If it was just your grandmother, this whole farm would be mine by now. I'd own every inch of Copper Lake."

"It's a good thing I'm around, then, isn't it?"

"That's a matter of opinion." He was close enough to share his unwanted body heat now. Another centimeter closer and she'd be falling onto the mattress where the dead woman had lain. "You want me to tell the police or KCFD that you were in here poking around—"

"You're trespassing, O'Brien." Mark Taylor's deep voice uttered a succinct warning from the open doorway.

O'Brien grinned at Amy's gasp of relief before turning. "Well, if it isn't the boyfriend."

Mark flashed his KCFD ID badge in his wallet and waved Amy over to stand beside him. She hurried around O'Brien as fast as her bruised ankle allowed. Mark caught her by the arm and pushed her behind him without taking his eyes off the bullying contractor. "Get out of here before I call the cops," he warned. "I have several of them on speed dial."

O'Brien chuckled. "You need to keep a shorter leash on your wild-child girlfriend, Taylor. She's messin' with things that don't belong to her." He held out the box and rattled the remaining contents. "Neither of you have any legal claim to whatever's inside this box."

Mark's hands fisted at his sides. "Your other option is for me to lay you out flat. And after the way I've seen you talk to my mother and Amy, I would love to."

O'Brien's amusement faded as he considered the validity of Mark's threat. He wisely decided that Mark could make good on besting him in a fight. He hugged the box to his chest and put one hand up, placating Mark as he sidled past them. "Hold your horses there, Taylor. I don't want any trouble. I'm going. I've retrieved what belongs to me." He looked past Mark's shoulder to Amy. "But you may want to investigate who stole it from me in the first place."

"I never took anything from you," Amy argued. She reached around Mark, but his arm straightened across her stomach, keeping her back. She latched on to the sleeve of his T-shirt, instead, pleading with him. "I found it under the floorboards. You can't let him leave with that. It's important."

"Did you take that from Amy's property?" Mark demanded.

O'Brien moved toward the door, keeping his eyes on Mark as he held up the box. "It has my name on it, doesn't it?"

"But there's evidence," she insisted. Not that it had been legally obtained, but it had to help with the investigation, didn't it?

"Evidence of what?" O'Brien taunted. His smarmy smile returned. "Nothing you can prove, darlin'."

Mark glanced over the jut of his shoulder at her, silently asking how far she wanted him to push this. At least she still had a handful of photos left in her bag. Plus, the pictures on her phone. It was more than she'd had a few minutes ago. If O'Brien wanted to claim that box and incriminate himself, she'd let KCPD deal with his explanation. Amy squeezed Mark's arm, thanking him for giving her a choice. "I just want him to leave."

"Done." With a curt nod, Mark pointed to the door. "I'll show you out."

Mark followed at a measured pace as O'Brien clutched the box and hurried his steps. Amy retrieved her boot and sat on the floor to untie it and pull it over her tender ankle. A minute or two later, she heard an engine starting and the crunch of gravel, and assumed O'Brien was driving away.

When Mark strode back into the room, he was on his phone. "Yeah, Matt. If you and any of the other guys can come out here and keep an eye on things while we're gone, I'll owe you a solid. Thanks." He disconnected the call and knelt in front of her. "My brothers and a couple of my crewmates are going to set up a round-the-clock watch on your place. We won't leave until I know someone's here whom I trust." His hand settled on her knee as he scanned her from head to toe and back. "Should I ask why you're in the middle of a crime scene that was cordoned off by KCPD and the fire department last night?"

Jeans and a KCFD T-shirt didn't make his broad shoulders and stern jaw look any less authoritative than he did in his black uniform or decked out in his full bunker gear. But those smoky blue eyes spoke of caring and concern and a compassion that soothed the edges off her fear. She could talk to those eyes. "I saw someone was in here and came to check it out. Suddenly, it was Grand Central Station. Richie Sterling, Brad Frick, Dale O'Brien. Any one of them, or all of them, could have been looking for that box. Or something else the police missed. I had to see what was going on."

"You *had* to?" He moved his hand to cup the side of her face and then captured the copper braid that fell over her shoulder. "Are you injured?"

"Turned my ankle when I fell through the floor. Nothing serious."

He immediately went into paramedic mode, inspecting her ankle before determining she was probably going to live. When she didn't protest, he tied her boot for her. "Keep this on. This is the last place you want to be running around in stockinged feet."

"Mark, that's not important. Look what I found." She pulled up the pictures on her phone. "These were in that strongbox. I had already taken a few of them out. There was a homemade fire-starter kit there, too. Probably not enough to burn down a house, but enough to start something small. Here." She showed him the images on her phone. "Is that significant?"

"You're right. A cotton ball soaked in petroleum jelly wouldn't burn long enough to take down a house. But it does show that someone likes playing with fire." He considered something for a moment. "If you stuffed the lit cotton inside the gas tank of a car…"

"It would torch it, like Jocelyn's Jeep?" It had been totaled, just like the equipment shed.

Mark nodded.

"I found more." She pulled the loose photographs from her backpack, but Mark pushed them away when she tried to hand them to him.

"The fewer people who touch those, the better. Show me." Mark's expression turned grim as she thumbed through the photographs.

"I want to show these to the police, too. What do you think they mean?" Amy shook her head. "What am I saying? I know what they mean. I've felt like someone's been watching me on and off for a long time now, but I didn't know he was taking pictures."

Mark muttered a curse. "You think someone's been spying on you out here? For how long?" He reached for her hand. "Never mind." He pulled her to her feet and slipped his arm around her waist, pulling her hip against his. "Can you walk?" Amy nodded. She doubted she even needed his steadying support as she barely limped along beside him, but she wasn't about to push away his solid warmth and sheltering strength. Her ankle might be fine, but her knees were still shaking after that encounter with Dale O'Brien. "I'm going to put in a call to my uncle Josh or Cole at KCPD. My brothers Pike and Alex aren't detectives like they are. I want to find out how they think we should handle this. Are you the only one who's touched these photographs?"

They stepped out into the sunlight, and Amy breathed in the fresh air, and the clean, freshly showered maleness that was all Mark Taylor. "Since I've been here, yes."

"Do you have any big plastic bags at your

house?" She nodded. Mark opened the passenger door to his truck, spanned his hands around her waist and lifted her in.

"I guess you *can* pick me up." She was half teasing, remembering the threat he'd made the first time they'd met. But she was also thinking of the gentleness and caring behind all that strength.

He winked. "Wait until I throw you over my shoulder." But before she could respond to the flirtation or even smile at seeing the intensity of his protective mode ease a fraction, he had closed the door and jogged around the hood to climb in behind the wheel. It was a quick drive to the top of the driveway, and then Mark was at her door again, winding a supportive arm around her waist and helping her up the steps into the house. "Get me those bags," he ordered, taking her all the way into the kitchen when she told him their location. He set her backpack on the table and hovered around her while she opened the drawer and got him the requested items. "I've learned enough from my brothers and uncles about police work to know that we shouldn't be touching things they might be able to get fingerprints from. While I'm doing this, you change your clothes and get your grandmother ready. Unless you need me to help you?"

Amy shook her head. "I can manage just fine. But I don't think Gran's awake yet."

"Then get her up. We're all going into the city this morning."

"Why?"

"Why? Because I'm not leaving any woman out here alone with that piece of scum O'Brien and everything else that's going on. I've got a place she can stay for a couple of hours while you and I are talking to the detectives."

"Okay." She made it to the kitchen archway before she stopped and turned. "Mark?"

He paused in his bagging of those disturbing pictures. "What is it?"

"I had a plan to get away from O'Brien."

"I'm sure you did."

"I'm strong and I'm smart. Maybe braver than I should be. I don't need you to rescue me." He set the bag down on the table and turned to argue something about being alone and getting hurt and somebody needed the hell to keep an eye on her. But his words fell silent when she crossed the room and wound her arms around his waist. Her forehead nestled in at the crook of his neck and collarbone, and she turned her ear to the strong beat of his heart. "But I do need you to hold me."

She felt the tension in him vanish as his strong arms folded around her and pulled her close. "Anytime, Red." He nuzzled his lips against her temple. "I will hold you anytime."

They stood together like that for countless moments until the warmth of Mark's body seeped into hers, chasing away the chill that even the summer day hadn't been able to reach. "I was scared," she confessed, knowing she was in a safe place to share the truth. "Of Brad and Richie. The timing was just so weird. I hate to give the man any kind of satisfaction, but I was scared of O'Brien, too. I'm scared of whoever took those pictures. I don't know who I should be afraid of, but I am."

"I know, Red. I know. Your last text scared me, too." He rubbed warm circles against her back, then settled his hand with a possessive familiarity over the curve of her hip. "And then I walked in and saw he'd cornered you against the back wall—"

"I wasn't giving up without a fight."

"Neither was I." When he started to pull away, Amy whimpered a protest. But the sound quickly became a groan of pleasure as Mark framed her face between his hands and kissed her. Deeply. Thoroughly. And far too briefly for a woman who was learning to love and trust this man more and more with every passing moment. She clung to his wrists as he leaned his forehead against hers. "Don't worry about the box O'Brien took. We'll get this guy with or without it. I just need you to be safe. Because, as far as I'm concerned, you are the only thing that's important."

Chapter Twelve

It didn't hurt that Mark's oldest uncle, Mitch Taylor, was the chief of police.

After a phone call to his uncle Josh to ask how Amy should handle this meeting with Detectives Beck and Carson, Mark dropped Comfort Hall off at his grandmother's house. Although Amy seemed inclined to stay a little longer and chat after he'd made the introductions, he'd reminded her of the time, dropped a quick kiss onto Martha Taylor's cheek and hurried Amy back to his truck, leaving the two older women standing in the front door of Martha Taylor's new house.

Josh must have mentioned something to Mitch because a phone call straight from the chief's office had suddenly changed Cathy Beck's doubting demeanor. While her partner, Dean Carson, copied the pictures off Amy's phone and took the photographs and Jocelyn's laptop into evidence, Detective Beck started treating Amy more like a witness than a suspect, jotting down notes of

Amy's account of this morning's events at the burned-out house and her run-in with Derek Roland on the Williams University campus. They agreed that the arson fires and murders were connected, although it would require more digging to determine if the murders were the reason the fires had been set, or the fires were the reason the murders had happened. Or, as Detective Beck postulated, was the killer taking advantage of some firebug's handiwork? Motive seemed to be the key to solving these crimes. Apparently, the motives for setting a fire and killing an innocent woman were quite different. If they could pinpoint why these women were being targeted, or why the fires were all on Hall property, they could narrow down their suspect list.

Mark's fingers were going numb from clutching them into fists while Amy described Roland's erratic behavior toward her, and the way she'd confronted the two handymen and Dale O'Brien this morning. Someone with a sick, selfish plan had been watching Amy, taking pictures of her, possibly setting her up to be his next victim. And he hadn't been there to protect her from any of it. It wasn't until Amy reached across from her chair to rest her hand over his fist that he realized just how tense sitting through this meeting and feeling like he'd failed her was making him.

Muscles leaped beneath his skin at her intuitive touch, calming him, centering him. When he forced his hand to relax, she laced her fingers together with his, linking them together while she answered Detective Beck's last question. Now his fingers were tingling where she touched him. Probably just the nerves waking up from the tight grip he'd held for too long, but maybe because, well, it seemed this woman's touch had awakened a lot of things inside him.

He squeezed his hand gently around hers where it rested on his thigh, and wondered how in the hell he was ever going to save her when a) she insisted she didn't want to be rescued, and b) he needed her quirky caring and trusting touch to save *him*.

"Thank you, Ms. Hall, Mr. Taylor." Detective Beck stood up and circled around her desk to shake Amy's hand. Mark stood and shook her hand, as well. "Thanks for keeping an eye on her. Although, I wish you'd leave the detective work to Dean and me. Don't suppose I can stop you from poking around your own place, though, can I."

"Just keep me in the loop if you can," Amy said. "Jocelyn didn't have an enemy in the world. I really want whoever did that to her to pay."

"We'll do our best."

Before they headed back out to his truck, Amy went to use the restroom and Mark seized the opportunity to stop by the officers' lounge to pay a visit to his two oldest brothers. He accepted a cup of coffee and gave Pike and Alex a brief rundown of everything that had happened out at Copper Lake and Amy's home, and why they were here at precinct headquarters. Since he'd already called in favors from Matt and his Lucky 13 crew to watch the place while he was gone, he asked his KCPD brothers to help with something else.

Alex didn't typically carry a notepad on his SWAT uniform, so he scribbled himself a note on a paper napkin. "Sure. I'll make a couple of calls to verify that Preston Worth is still living in Montana."

"And hasn't shown his face in Kansas City anytime over the past few months."

"Hasn't…shown…his…face…" Alex copied the words and underlined them.

Pike doctored the bitter coffee with a shot of milk before bending his long legs and settling onto the vinyl couch. His K-9 partner, Hans, lay down at his feet. "You think this old boyfriend could be seeking retribution against Amy?"

Mark leaned against the door frame and downed half of the nasty brew. He'd been going almost forty-eight hours on just a couple of naps since his KCFD shift had started two days ago. He was off the clock now, but he didn't intend to crash and leave Amy alone without him guarding her back just because his stomach lining was tired of downing caffeine. "He's at the bottom of my suspect list. Those pictures tell me this killer is patient, calculating. The fires had to have been planned—the targets are specific to the old Hall farm, and we'd have somebody on our radar by now if anyone unfamiliar with the place was seen there. Worth sounds like a temper tantrum waiting to happen." Mark forced himself to take another sip. "But so help me, if that man does show his face anywhere near Amy, I'll have to ask you two to look the other way."

Alex grinned. "We'll let you have a punch or two before we arrest him for violating his no-contact order."

"It was an abusive relationship?" Pike asked, possibly remembering the trauma his wife had suffered growing up.

Mark nodded. "Amy told me he put her in the hospital. Then he tried to blackmail her into not reporting him."

"And he's the one who lost his job and ended up serving time." Alex raked his fingers through his dark curly hair and huffed a noise of admiration. "That woman sounds like she's got some backbone. Think you can handle her, baby brother?"

"I can handle her just fine," Mark answered, refusing to be baited by his teasing. "She says she needs me, and I don't intend to let her down."

"Hold on a minute." Pike braced his elbows on his knees and leaned forward. "Matt said you were struggling with some kind of savior complex because of Grandpa Sid. Taking risks you shouldn't, getting involved with a woman you barely know—"

"I *know* Amy in every way I need to." Mark straightened where he stood. He didn't have to defend his feelings for Amy, but he was doing it anyway. Because denying his feelings for her would be a lie. "I've talked more to Amy Hall in these past two weeks than I have to any other woman I dated for months. How long did you have to be with Hope…or Audrey—" he included Alex's wife in his argument, too "—before you knew you were in love with them?"

Tactical error! Mark saw the transformation from concerned argument to surprise to amusement at his expense on his brothers' faces.

"You're in love with her?" Pike asked. He and Alex exchanged a knowing look. "Uh-oh."

Mark crossed the room and tossed his empty coffee cup in the trash with more force than was necessary. "My point is, I'm not doing this for Amy because I feel guilty about Grandpa and I think I have to make amends. She needs somebody. She says she needs me. I want to be there for her."

"We're not questioning what's in your heart, baby bro." Alex moved in beside him, slapping a hand against his shoulder. "Well, not about Amy."

Why did Pike moving in on the other side of Mark make him feel like he was about to get some kind of intervention on his love life? "You didn't answer my question. Do you love her?"

Mark glanced up into blue eyes and down into brown before he answered. "How do you know?"

"You know," Alex assured him.

Pike's reply was more helpful. "Does anything scare you more than losing her?"

Mark squeezed his eyes shut and remembered the blinding anger he'd felt when he'd caught O'Brien trapping Amy in that burned-out bedroom. He remembered the utter destruction of an innocent life when they'd discovered Jocelyn Brunt's body and when he'd found Lissette Peterson dead, bound and burning in last night's fire. He remembered the angry bruises on Amy's hand and wrist and the pictures someone had taken of her, watching her, stalking her. His gut was tight with dread as he connected the dots and imagined some bastard breaking Amy's stubborn will and silencing that beautiful mouth.

Yeah. Losing Amy scared him more than anything.

"I love her."

Pike squeezed his shoulder. "She can't do any better than you, baby bro."

Alex squeezed the other shoulder. "We'll get this guy," he promised. "You're a Taylor. You'll keep her safe. We've got your back for whatever you need."

"Thanks."

And then, because they were brothers and they loved each other and they knew each other so well, Alex ended the supportive moment with a punch to Mark's shoulder. "Then, if you're not moping over this woman, and you're not feeling guilty about Grandpa Sid, why did you make Grandma cry?"

Mark groaned and shoved them both off. "This is not the time, Alex."

Pike stopped him at the door and showed him an old family picture in his wallet from when they were newly adopted kids. "See this picture? She's smiling. You made her cry, dude, by skipping her open house. You didn't even give her a reason why. Not cool."

"I've already had this conversation with Matt."

Alex nodded toward the curvy redhead coming down the hall to join them, but he had one more lick to get in before the conversation ended. "Then you know what you need to do to make it right."

Amy arched a questioning eyebrow as she walked up to the three of them. "Am I interrupting anything?"

Alex grinned. "I see what's to like, Mark. Nicely done."

"Excuse me?" Amy was an only child. She had no idea how relentless the teasing among a team of brothers could be.

Mark reached for her hand and pulled her into

the break room. "Red, these are my brothers Alex and Pike."

He knew when she touched her necklace that she was a little anxious about this introduction. She was grounding herself, reminding herself she could deal with this. And she could do it with her beautiful smile. "Wow. Uncles? Brothers? Are you related to every cop in Kansas City?"

Alex, who was shorter than she was, took her other hand and winked. "Just the good-lookin' ones like me."

Pike nudged Alex aside to shake her hand, as well. "Ignore him. He's married, adopting a baby and not nearly as charming as he thinks he is. I'm Pike Taylor. Beautiful wife. Two kids. Big dog. I'm the brains of the family."

"You wish." Alex shoved him right back.

"You two work this out on your own time." Mark slid his hand behind Amy's waist, steering her toward the elevators. "We have to go."

"Nice to meet you, Amy," Pike called after them.

"Talk to Grandma, Mark." Alex was more direct as he followed them to the elevators. "I can't handle her crying over you because you skipped her party, and she thinks you're avoiding her."

Several minutes later, Mark and Amy were in his truck, cruising onto the highway toward his grandmother's house east of downtown KC. Mark was deep in thought, about Grandpa Sid, about his brothers' concern that he was alienating the one family member he loved the most, about his feelings for Amy.

Probably because his brooding radiated off him and filled up the truck cab, Amy reached over to adjust the air-conditioning and broke the silence. "Wow. Your brothers are sure protective of your grandmother. Saving the day seems to be a trait that runs in your family."

He grunted. She was tapping into a well of emotions he wasn't sure he could keep a cap on anymore.

"Why didn't you go to the party?" she asked. "Did you have to work?"

Mark's fingers tightened on the steering wheel. He felt her eyes on his hands, knew she had some kind of weird fascination with men's hands and wondered what message she was getting from his white-knuckled grip.

They'd pulled off on the exit to Lee's Summit Road before Amy spoke again. "Is this about your grandfather's death?"

"Don't you push, too." The cap had been opened, and the emotions were steaming to the top.

"If you haven't noticed, that's kind of my nature. You're hurting. Apparently, she's hurting, too, if your brothers are that worried." Her gaze darted between his eyes and his hands. "If you want to stay for a while and talk to her, I don't mind. Gran and I can wait in the truck."

Mark shook his head and turned south. "I want

you and Comfort to stay with Grandma. At least for a night or two. One of my uncles or brothers can be there to keep an eye on you. You and I should go back to your house to pack some things for her. I'll stop by my place on the way back and pack a bag so I can stay out at the farm. I don't think we should leave it unattended."

"One, no one is chasing me out of my own home. And two, do you feel responsible for your grandfather's death?"

"What?" The truck swerved toward the next lane as his hands jerked on the wheel. That vat of emotion was completely uncorked now. "I *am* responsible." He wasn't sure if it was his brothers' badgering or the fact that he'd already shared so much with Amy that he felt he could talk to her about anything. He pounded the steering wheel as the guilt and pain came pouring out. "You've seen a glimpse of what a big, loving, crazy family I have. I took him away from all that."

"Did you murder him?"

"What? Of course not. He had a heart attack. We were…" He shook his head. His jaw hurt because of how tightly he was clenching it. "I don't want you to see me hurt and angry like this. I don't want you to ever be afraid of me."

"Pull off into that parking lot, Mark. We need to talk." Oh, man, she was tough. On the outside. But he knew how vulnerable she could be, too. She pointed to the next turnoff. "Do it, Fire Man."

He glanced across the seat. If she had on that bossy, let's-run-into-the-fire look on her face, he would keep driving. Instead, she looked frightened, sad. She cared that he was hurting. He couldn't resist the woman who looked at him with those hazel eyes as though she believed he could make her world better.

Slowing the truck, he pulled up beside an empty ball field in Adair Park. Before he'd even turned off the engine, she was unbuckling and climbing onto her seat. She reached across the center console and placed her hands over his, gently willing him to let go—of the steering wheel and of the guilt and pain battling inside him. "For what it's worth, you are too kind, too Captain Good Guy, for me ever to be afraid of you, Fire Man. Now talk."

He pulled her hands to his lips and kissed them. She waited patiently for Mark to unfasten his seat belt and push his seat all the way back. She didn't protest when he reached across the truck to pull her onto his lap. With her long legs stretched out across the console, she wound one arm around his neck and stroked the angles of his cheek and jaw with gentle fingertips. Although the sweet weight of her hip nestled against his groin stirred other ideas, he reveled in her tender ministrations. She was warm and caring and strong and irresistible. Mark felt the hard shell that guarded his emotions crack open and crumble into dust.

Maybe she was right about the whole rescuing thing. *He* was the one who needed to be rescued. *He* was the one who needed to trust that his heart and his secrets and his future would be safe with *her*.

After several moments of simply touching her hair and putting his faith in those green-gold eyes, Mark drew his hand down the smooth skin of her neck to capture the chain she always wore between his fingers. He traced the path of the chain down to the pendant of knotted silver around a small heart and treasured the warmth it had drawn from her skin into his palm. The symbolism of trusting Amy with his own heart and all its twisty complications wasn't lost on him. She had made this beautiful thing. She had made his heart come alive again.

And she still waited for him to speak.

"Grandpa and I were…" He hated to say the touchy word around her, but she wanted the truth. "We were *rescuing* some people from a bad car accident. The strain was too much for his heart." Her sympathetic gasp couldn't stop him now. The comfort of her hand stroking his jaw couldn't stop him, either. "I saved everyone else that day. Didn't save the one man who mattered the most."

"Was he as old as Martha?"

"A couple years older. Why?"

Her fingers trailed down his neck to rest against his chest. "My grandfather was seventy-nine when he passed. His doctor said every heart has only so many beats in it. Whether you were helping those people who needed you or not, maybe his heart was done. It was his time."

He released the pendant and curled his hand around the curve of her thigh. "Great. So, you're saying he would have died in my truck driving home from the lake. *Still* my watch."

"You need to talk to your grandmother about all this, Mark. You're both grieving. Instead of fighting each other, you could be healing each other."

"It hurts."

"Hell yes, it hurts." She slipped her arms around his neck and hugged him tightly, briefly, before sitting back in his lap. Her hands framed his jaw. "I was in the middle of Preston's trial when my grandfather died. You don't think I wanted to be there for him? You don't think I felt guilty that all my trouble caused him so much stress that it probably contributed to his heart attack?"

He rubbed his hand up to her bottom and down to her knee, wanting to draw her even closer. "You didn't tell me that's how you lost him. I'm sorry."

"Look, Mark, I know I'm not the poster child for smart choices and easy answers, but I do know about surviving. I know about all the fear and guilt and grief that goes along with that." She stroked her fingers across his lips, and he felt the tugging need to kiss her all the way down to his groin. "The number one thing I've learned is to be with the people who love you the most. When Grandpa Leland died, Gran needed me. She didn't need me wallowing in self-pity. She needed someone to take care of. She needed someone to grieve with who understood just how much it hurts to lose someone you love. She needed someone to love when Grandpa Leland died. So did I. So do you." Tears glistened in her eyes, but she blinked them away before Mark's thumb could catch one. "Getting over a loss like this—it's not going to fix itself overnight. But it will get better. I promise. If you're anything like your grandfather, I know he was a good man. I can imagine the loss you feel. Let your grandmother take care of you a little bit. Let her talk and share memories. And you do the same. Don't deny her—or you—the chance to heal together."

When her fingers tried to brush his hair into order, the last of Mark's strength snapped. He crushed Amy in his arms, buried his nose in the herbal scent of her hair and finally shed the tears that had been locked up inside him.

Her arms circled around him and held him tight as she whispered soft comforts against his ear and gently rocked him. Mark shook with the depth of his grief. He released some of his guilt into the depth of her strength. And still she held on.

He loved this woman so much. He needed her. He wanted her. Whether it was yin and yang, Captain Good Guy and the bad girl, intuitive and creative and grounded in training and duty, she completed him. Amy Hall made Mark Taylor whole again. This woman who had seemed so alone knew more about being together with him than he ever knew he needed.

Somewhere along the way, the intensity of his emotions turned to passion, and the generosity of her comfort turned to a blinding need to know all of her.

Mark seized her mouth in a searing kiss that ignited a fire behind his eyes and in his heart and in that potent male part of him that wanted to link them together in the most elemental way. After a quick scan outside to assure the privacy of their surroundings, Mark tilted his seat back as far as it would go and pulled Amy on top of him.

He palmed the back of her head and squeezed her bottom, fitting her to him in all the right places. He thrust his tongue in her mouth and traded sparks of desire, claiming and taking as equal partners. His jeans grew uncomfortably tight as her thighs settled on either side of him and gripped his hips. Her breasts were beautiful, pillowy mounds that flattened against his chest, her nipples beady pearls that branded him through the clothes they still wore.

Too many clothes, too tight a space, perfect

woman, consuming need. Not the way he'd imagined making love to Amy. But he had a will, and he would make a way. He cupped her hips and lifted her slightly off him, loving how she arched to keep their lips together even as he unbuttoned her blouse and filled his hand with a full perfect breast. He caught the tip between his thumb and hand and she finally tore her mouth from his and gasped a hot, breathy moan. "Not fair, Fire Man. This is supposed to be a two-way… I want to…"

When he unhooked her bra and moved her to capture the pale pink tip in his mouth, he discovered she had trouble saying any words at all. She hummed. She moaned. She made him crazy, kissing and nibbling on any part of him she could reach. Her fingers tightened against his scalp when he moved her to claim the other breast.

She knew where this was going because she uttered a single word—"Protection?"—before tugging at the hem of his T-shirt and scorching her hands across his flank and chest.

"Are you sure?" A rational part of his brain tried to fight its way through the fire raging inside him. She unzipped him and her hand found its way inside his jeans to cup him, and Mark discovered he was the one struggling to talk. "Can't…be…too…good here."

"With you, it'll be perfect." He guided her hand to the back pocket of his jeans and she pulled out his billfold. "We'll do it pretty next time."

"Next time. I like that."

"Shut up, Fire Man." Together, they opened the condom, pushed aside jeans, shorts and panties. Mark cracked his knee on the steering column, but barely felt it. Amy's elbow hit the automatic door lock the next time he lifted her. "Soon. Now."

And then he lowered her on top of him. She was hot, wet, perfect. Her moans were music to his ears. Her greedy hands roaming all over him were incendiary. Once they were linked as closely as a man and woman could be, Mark thrust inside her. Her soft, freckled breasts bobbed in his face as they found the rhythm they needed to bring each other to a swift, fiery completion. As Mark released himself on one last, powerful thrust, he slipped his thumb between them to tease her sensitive bundle of nerves and ignite the tremors that cascaded all around him. "Yep. Great…hands…" Overcome by the strength of her release, she gasped his name and collapsed on top of him.

Mark wrapped his arms around Amy and whispered, "You're beautiful."

A few minutes later, spurred by the reality of all they needed to do and the possibility that they might be discovered, despite the empty parking lot and trees that blocked his truck and the ball field from the road, Mark sat up, spilling Amy into his lap. She scrambled over the console and

Mark straightened his seat. He put the condom back into its wrapper and dropped it into the trash while she adjusted her clothes and combed her fingers through the loose hair he'd pulled from her braid.

"Well, that was cathartic," she teased, buttoning up her blouse. She'd missed a hole and was buttoning it crooked, reminding him just how sweet and sexy and desirable she was. When he pointed it out, her face turned an endearing shade of pink and she started again. "I don't think I've ever been that…spontaneous."

"You?" Not that Mark was having an easy time getting his shorts straightened inside his jeans again. "I figured you were the adventurous type."

"I've only been with one other man, and that didn't turn out the way I—"

He pressed a finger over her kiss-stung lips and tried to make that memory recede. "I'm sorry. Forget about him. I'm sorry he hurt you. But I'm glad he's gone so you can be here with me now."

"Me, too." She reached across the seat and feathered her fingers through his hair, trying to make him look presentable, too. "With Preston, the emotion wasn't there. I realize that now. It's a lot more intense when I believe the guy wants me, and just me."

"Believe it." He caught her hand and pressed a kiss to her fingers before releasing her to fasten his seat belt and start the engine. "You'd better tone down the blush on your cheeks so our grand-mothers don't guess what we've been doing."

"I'll stop blushing if you will."

No doubt. Even though his emotions had been tempered and his desire temporarily quenched, he was still hot for this woman. "I am in love with you, Amy Hall."

She settled back in her seat and buckled up. "Now, *that* scares me."

"It shouldn't. You're the bravest woman I know. I would never pressure you to jump into something you're not ready for. And I would never hurt you the way your professor did."

"I know that. What scares me is that I think I'm in love with you, too."

Mark reached across the seat to take her hand, holding on tight to his future.

Now, if they could track down an arsonist turned serial killer, he and Amy might just have a chance to make that future happen.

Chapter Thirteen

After his *conversation* with Amy, it was surprisingly easy to sit down at the kitchen table with Martha Taylor and apologize for distancing himself from his grandmother. Her bony, arthritic hand, marked by age spots and years of hard work, never left his as she gently clasped his fingers across the table.

Mark was beginning to understand Amy's fascination with hands. They said so much about a person. Strength, gentleness. A link of family and trust. Shared history and new feelings. A loving touch versus a hurtful one. He had an affinity for certain hands, too. Like the freckled hand that eased his pain and stoked his desire. Like the one holding his now.

"It's my job to save people. I didn't save him."

"You didn't let your grandfather die," Martha insisted. "He didn't think that and neither do I."

Mark shook his head, wishing he could make things right. "I was running around while he was making like the Hulk, pulling equipment out of the truck and taking care of that baby. I was so busy taking care of everybody else and putting out that fire that I wasn't paying any attention to his distress. I took him for granted, Grandma."

She turned her blue eyes to the sunlight streaming through the kitchen window for a moment before she sighed and faced him again. "You mean, you took it for granted that my Sid was always going to be there for you?"

"Don't get into semantics about generations and life spans. I should have saved him. I should have been there for him when he needed me most. And I wasn't."

He could never argue that his grandmother wasn't a wise, intuitive woman. "So, you've been avoiding me because you feel guilty? I thought maybe you were afraid that I was going to leave you, too. That you were mad at us for being old and no longer the vibrant, fun-loving grands you could do no wrong with."

"Mad?" Mark was stunned that she'd even considered him feeling that way. "I love you. Come on. I'm your baby boy. You know that."

"I do." The teakettle on the stove whistled, and he waited patiently while she got up and poured the water into a teapot and carried it and a tray of cups back to the table. "Your grandfather had a serious heart event fifteen years ago. I nearly lost him then. Sid and I both knew that he was living on borrowed time—and he was determined to make the most of that precious gift of a second life. He wanted to live and love and laugh and see his grandsons grow into fine young men." Standing beside Mark, she cupped his cheek. The tears in her eyes would have gutted him until he realized she was smiling. "I am grateful beyond measure to know that he had you with him when he died. That he wasn't alone. That he left this world doing something important, saving lives. That he had the grandson he loved so well and was so proud of with him at the end. It helps me know that he died a happy man." Mark hadn't thought he had any tears left in him, but when they spilled over, his grandmother wiped them away and pressed a kiss to his cheek. "Thank you for being with him, Mark. Thank you for that precious gift."

"Ah, Grandma." Mark pushed to his feet and wrapped her up in his arms.

She hugged him back. "That's what I needed. A big bear hug from my favorite grandson."

"Favorite? You say that to all of us."

Her frail arms tightened around him for a precious moment before she relaxed against him. "I do. Take it or leave it," she teased.

"I'll take it." They laughed together. "I miss him, Grandma. I miss him so much."

"I miss him, too." After a few moments, she pulled away, brushing a few last tears from her cheeks. "But do you know how angry he'd be if he thought you were throwing your life away? Taking unnecessary risks? Refusing to live and love and laugh the way he wanted you to?" A stern matriarchal finger poked the middle of his chest. "Do you know how hurt I'll be if I lose you, too?"

She curled a finger, urging him to follow her over to the cabinets. "I don't remember my birth parents. But I do remember being lost, and a little scared of the world until Mom and Dad adopted Matt and me—Alex and Pike, too. When I found out you and Grandpa were part of the deal, I was on cloud nine. Being the youngest of four brothers, though, I got lost in the shuffle sometimes. But Grandpa—and you—always had time for me."

She opened the cabinet and set four plates in his hands. "Those are the memories you need to cherish, Mark. It's okay to be sad. But don't waste time with regrets."

"That's about what Amy said."

"Sounds like a smart girl." She handed him silverware and napkins and ushered him back to the table. Somehow, Martha Taylor was one step ahead of him. "Now, where is that young woman of yours? If she's half as fun as Comfort is, I need to get to know her."

"She's a little different, Grandma."

"Good. That means she's interesting." After

the table was set, she nudged him toward the back door, where he'd left Amy and her grandmother inspecting the contents of Martha's late summer garden. "Go. Invite her in. You and the Hall women are all having lunch with me today."

"I'd like that." Mark grinned and kissed the top of her head. "I love you, Grandma."

"I love you, too. Oh, and, Mark?" She stopped him with his hand on the doorknob and touched her fingers to her white hair. "Maybe you and Amy should comb your hair after you…enjoy each other's company."

"Grandma!"

Hell. Nothing got past that woman.

She chuckled. "I think your grandfather would have liked her, too."

Mark knew he was blushing when he stepped outside.

ONCE THEY TURNED off the highway and slowed their speed to drive through the hills toward Copper Lake, Amy cracked open the window of Mark's truck and breathed in the hazy air. It smelled of dried grass, pungent earth and asphalt, but there was something about the chill of the truck's air-conditioning, or maybe it was the idea of returning home to where innocent women died and creeps spied on her that left her shivering.

"You doing okay?" Mark asked, slowing as

they drove through the Copper Lake subdivision and construction zone.

Amy's gaze zeroed in on Dale O'Brien's office trailer and the familiar company truck parked out front. Brad Frick's car was there, too, making her wonder what connection the men shared—why they'd all been in that burned house this morning, why they'd been so anxious to get her out of there. Were they just three slimy, opportunistic morons? Or did they share a more sinister connection?

Brad leaned against the car, flicking away a cigarette as they drove past. Amy curled her fingers through Mark's when she felt his touch on the back of her hand. "So much has changed today."

"Some of it for the good, I hope."

She nodded and faced the much more pleasurable scenery of Mark's angular face. "Of course. I don't regret what happened between us. I'm just not sure if I'm ready for what happens next. We haven't even been on a real date yet."

He turned north to circle the lake. "What happens next is we pack a bag for Comfort. I might not be able to convince you to leave, but at least she'll be safe, spending a few nights with my grandmother. Then I'll grab my bag and bunk on your couch until this guy is caught. That date will happen. I promise."

"Is he going to go into hiding or leave town if you're here with me?"

"I'm not setting you up as bait to draw this guy out."

"I don't know if I can handle another murder," she confessed. "I'm not even sure I can handle another fire. O'Brien has to be behind it somehow."

Mark released her to turn into the gravel driveway and pulled up beside his brother Matt's truck. "The detectives are already on his case and have subpoenaed him to turn over that strongbox you found this morning."

"It's probably long gone. At the bottom of the lake or buried somewhere else."

"Then they'll arrest him for obstruction of justice." He set the brake and shut off the engine. "Either way, he won't be getting close to you again. Not while I'm around."

Yeah, but would Mark always be around to rescue her? He had to go to work sometime. He'd have family events to attend. And was what they were feeling really love? Or *love for now* because she'd helped him past an emotional hurdle, her situation fed his Captain Good Guy genes and the chemistry between them was undeniably hot?

Amy nodded, wishing she could see things in black-and-white as clearly as Mark apparently did. She knew just how complicated relationships could get. And while she truly believed he would never physically hurt her, would Mark tire of the drama she brought to his life?

"You are not the introspective type," Mark said, waiting to open his door until she gave him an answer he liked. "So, get out of your head and start talking to me."

"I'm just tired." It wasn't a lie. She'd been through a physical and emotional wringer today. "I'm tired of having to keep fighting. I'm already tired of the fight that I know is ahead of us." She pointed to the big man getting out of his truck and circling around to greet them. "Let's see what Matt has to say."

"Amy." Mark captured her hand before she got out the door. "Like I said before, you're strong. You're my grandmother kind of strong."

She smiled. "That's a nice compliment, Fire Man."

But she wasn't sure she believed it.

Without so much as a hello, Matt Taylor stuck his fingers into the back pockets of his jeans and launched into a concise report. "Nobody's been in or out that front door since I got here. Your neighbor left after four o'clock. Only people I've seen have been the workmen across the lake. There was another car out here. Driver had long blond hair. He drove off in a rush as soon as I got out of my truck to talk to him."

"Derek Roland." Amy shoved her fingers through her hair and rubbed the tension gathering at the base of her skull. "Maybe he came to apologize."

Mark slipped his hand beneath her braid to take over the quick massage. "Or to find out what the police said about him stealing your friend's laptop."

That was a more likely scenario. And certainly, someone built like Matt Taylor with his spooky impassive glare would be more than enough of a threat to send a man like Derek scurrying back to whatever hole he'd crawled out of. "I'd better get Gran's suitcase out." She squeezed Matt's sturdy forearm as she moved past him. "Thank you for keeping an eye on things."

The glare softened with the hint of a smile. Matt tipped his head toward Mark. "You keep an eye on this one."

The change in Matt's expression felt like a hard-won seal of approval.

Amy smiled. "I will."

As Amy headed up the porch steps and unlocked the front door, she overheard Matt's words to his brother. "I hear you squared things with Grandma."

"We talked."

"Good man."

Apparently, *that* was another form of approval from Matt. And a goodbye. But Amy's attention had already shifted with concern as the two brothers shook hands and Matt climbed into his truck and drove away.

Amy was waiting inside the foyer when she heard Mark jogging up the steps behind her. Her eyes had started watering as soon as she'd stepped inside. She frowned at the haze hanging in the air. Something acrid stung her eyes and nose. "Brad and Richie must have left one of the stain cans open."

When she ducked beneath the scaffolding to check the sawhorses where they stored their tools and refinishing supplies, Mark grabbed her arm and jerked her back behind him. "That's not an open can of paint." A muscle ticked along his jaw as he tilted his nose into the air and sniffed. "Something's burning."

"What?" The tension she felt in his grip radiated through her. She looked up the stairs and around the foyer, searching for flames and smoke. "Are you sure?"

When she looked back at Mark, his eyes were focused on the landing above them. "Up there. Could be electrical. Could be some kind of delayed ignition. And we just fed it an influx of oxygen when we opened that front door. It's probably been smoldering since early this morning, before Matt got here. He never came inside, so he never noticed it." He crossed to the bottom of the stairs, pulling her with him. The haze at the top of the stairs was thicker, a swirling mist of grays that grew darker toward the ceiling. "Smoke will fill the upper levels first. It's had all day to work its way down to the first floor. What's up there?"

"Bedrooms. A guest bathroom."

"Is there an attic?"

Amy nodded. "You access it through the closet in my bedroom. On the far right."

Mark pulled her into a quick jog beside him as he ran back outside. "Come on. I've got a fire extinguisher in my truck."

He vaulted into the bed of his truck and unlocked the metal storage unit there. "Call 9-1-1. Tell them there's a second-story or attic fire. I won't know for sure until I find the source." Fire extinguisher in hand, he jumped down to the gravel and reached around her to open the driver's-side door. "Get in."

"You're not going back in there."

Just like he had this morning, he lifted her onto the seat. "Firefighter, Red. If I can put it out or contain it, I will. If not, help will already be on the way."

He pushed the door lock and closed it. Amy didn't waste any time playing the damsel in distress. The moment he turned his back, she shoved the door open again. "Shouldn't you wait for backup? Bad things happen in fires around here. At least let me come with you."

Three strides brought him back to the open truck door. "I can't be worrying about you *and* the fire. I'm not the one someone's been spying on. Stay safe. Lock yourself in." He pushed his phone into her hand. "Find my brother Matt's number and call him back here. He can be here faster than Firehouse 13." Amy nodded, already pulling out her own phone to dial 9-1-1. Before she could place either call, he reached through the open door, palmed the back of her head and pulled her to him for a quick, hard kiss. "I love you. Lock the doors. Call."

Then he was running back into the house. Amy remembered him bursting through the flames with Lissette Peterson in his arms. He'd been in full turnout gear that night. Jeans, a T-shirt and fire extinguisher were hardly enough protective equipment if he came across another woman he had to rescue.

Swallowing her fears and saying a prayer for his safety, Amy scrolled through his phone and found Matt's number. He picked up on the second ring. "Miss me, baby bro?"

"Matt? Amy Hall here. There's a fire somewhere upstairs in the house. Mark said to call you for backup. He's already inside. I don't want him in there alone."

She heard tires screeching on the pavement. Matt's reply was as reassuring as it was brief. "On my way."

Amy didn't take her eyes off the house as she dialed 9-1-1 and reported the fire to the dispatcher. The early evening sun reflected like inlaid gold off the top-floor windows as she visually imagined Mark charging up the stairs and searching through every room and the attic until he located the source of the fire he'd detected.

She'd just tilted her gaze to the open ventilation slats in the attic just below the peak of the roofline when one of those gold windows shattered and rained shards of glass down on the porch roof and ground below. "Oh, my God." The flames she'd been searching for earlier shot out through the broken window, like billowing arms reaching out for the oxygen it craved. She knew Mark was fit and fast, but he hadn't flown up the stairs and couldn't have reached her bedroom that quickly. "Mark?"

"Ma'am?"

"I see flames now," she reported to the dispatcher. "Second-story front window. Mark Taylor is inside. He's an off-duty firefighter. Send help. Send lots of help."

Someone else was in the house with the man she loved. She looked at the two phones in her hands. She couldn't call him and warn him.

She'd do it herself.

"Send the police, too!" Amy yelled before hanging up and stuffing both phones into her pockets. She dashed up the stairs and shoved open the door. A wave of smoke washed over her, filling her lungs and eyes. "Mark!" She coughed her lungs clear and ran to the bottom of the stairs. "Fire Man! He's here! He's already in the house with you!"

She heard a thud and a grunt and something metal and heavy rolling across the landing floor. "Mark?"

Fear propelled her up the first few steps, but she halted when she saw movement in the smoke above her. She squinted to bring the ghostly figures she saw moving through the smoke into focus. Two men. Was one carrying the other away from the smoke and flames? Were they fighting?

Before she fully understood what was happening, she saw Mark's inert body fold over the railing like a rag doll. "Mark!"

He hit the top level of the scaffolding with a smack and then the framework of metal tilted forward, wobbling, tipping, until the whole thing toppled over and crashed into the foyer. Amy jumped back against the wall as boards and metal poles and tools and cans hurtled down to the floor, bounced, broke apart and collapsed into a pile of burning tarps and dust and smoke.

"Mark!"

No, no, no, no, no! He couldn't be dead. Not her Fire Man. Amy raced down the stairs and climbed into the destruction, stepping where she could, flinging aside debris and crawling underneath the mangled scaffolding where she couldn't. She found Mark buried in the middle of it all.

Lying so still. She bent over him to see blood oozing from a wound at the side of his head. She put her hand over his heart. It was beating, strong, fast. He'd taken a horrible blow to the head and was knocked out cold. There was a tear in his jeans where he was bleeding from a cut. But he was alive. *Please, God. Stay alive!*

"This is not how we're going to end," she vowed, rising to her feet and kicking aside the burning tarp that had landed near his feet. She could see the shiny gleam of the liquid someone had poured over it, liquid that disappeared as the flames drank up the flammable chemical. She was seriously coughing now, struggling to take in a full breath of air, but she was breathing. And as long as she was alive, she would fight. For this man, for her grandmother, for Jocelyn and the other women—she would fight. She curled her arms beneath his shoulders and pushed with her legs, pulling him away from the brightest of the flames, dragging him through the foyer toward the front door and fresh air.

All that breadth and strength she loved when he was awake and holding her now pulled against her like dead weight. She screamed with the exertion of dragging him to safety. When she butted against a cage-like wall of broken scaffolding, she set him down as gently as she could and shoved with all her might against it. Her eyes were burning and watering so badly now, she could barely see. She could barely catch her breath. She leaned over him to touch his heart and make sure he was still alive before summoning the last of her strength and rising to push the debris aside, since she couldn't pick him up and carry him over it.

· She grunted as she pushed, then stumbled to the floor as the section of scaffolding suddenly rose into the air and flew into the stairs. What was happening? Had Matt arrived? Was someone here to help her?

Amy was looking at a scuffed pair of men's work boots when she pushed herself up onto her elbows. "He's hurt. We have to get him out…"

The man upstairs. Mark hadn't been alone.

She scrambled onto her bottom and scooted away, wanting to protect Mark from the man she guessed had pushed him over the railing. "Stay away from him." Her words were a feeble croak that scratched through her throat and triggered another coughing fit. "You didn't have to hurt him. Is it me you want?"

A scraped and bruised hand reached down to help her stand.

Amy followed the arm up to the man's face.

Sunburned cheeks puffed up as the man smiled down at her.

"I don't understand. Richie?" Brad Frick's friendly, simpleminded sidekick.

Not help. A killer. Jocelyn's killer.

When she didn't take his hand, he squatted

in front of her. His tone was as friendly as ever. "I've got a special place all set up for us in your art studio."

"My studio? Us?" Why wasn't this making any sense? "Did you take pictures of me, Richie? Do you like taking pictures of women?"

"Yeah. Pretty women. I like them."

Amy's skin crawled. There was something wrong in this man's head, something she doubted she could reason with. "Did you take pictures of my friend Jocelyn? And Lissette over at the construction site? Did you kill them?"

"Stop talking. Walk with me." He grabbed her arm.

Amy shrugged him off and crawled to Mark's body, willing him to wake up, wanting to tell him she loved him, wondering if she had any chance of living through this night. Other than the blood on his head and leg, he looked as though he was sleeping. And she might never see his beautifully interesting face or feel his strong arms around her again.

"Miss Amy," Richie prompted. "You belong to me. I want you." He coughed behind her. Odd. Somehow, she'd expected an arsonist to be immune to smoke and fire. "The fire will hide my mistake," he said, as though burning Mark's body would be a reassurance to her. "Mr. O'Brien paid Brad and me to set fires. I liked it. Brad liked the money, but I thought it was fun. Now I use them to hide my mistakes."

Jocelyn was a mistake. Lissette was a mistake. Now Mark—and maybe she, too—would be the latest mistake covered up by Richie Sterling's fires.

"I won't leave him," she protested, hoping she could order Richie away from whatever he had planned. "You'll have to go without me."

"That's not how it works." He whined a little like a frustrated child who hadn't gotten his way. "I want you to walk with me to your studio."

Amy's pendant fell out of the neckline of her blouse and dangled in front of her as she bent over Mark. Her studio. She caught the pendant in her hand and tugged the chain from around her neck. Matt Taylor and the rest of Firehouse 13 were coming. She just had to stay alive long enough for help to arrive. Long enough for Mark to wake up and do his Captain Good Guy thing.

"Rescue me, Fire Man," she whispered against his ear before she pressed a kiss there and slipped her necklace into the pocket of his jeans.

Richie's hand clamped down around her upper arm in a bruising grip and he pulled Amy to her feet. She shoved at his chest and struggled against him. "I don't want to be another one of your mistakes. Richie, you have to let me go."

"Walk." He held up the mallet he must have struck Mark with. Blood dripped from the tip onto the antique oak floor. "Or I'll hit him again."

Chapter Fourteen

Mark was regaining consciousness as his brother Matt hauled him onto his shoulders and carried him from the burning house.

As soon as he laid him on the ground outside, Mark rolled onto his hands and knees, coughing the smoke and chemicals from his lungs and drawing in deep breaths of pure oxygen from the breathing mask, which Matt held over his nose and mouth. Ball bearings pinged back and forth inside his skull with every cough. But once his vision had cleared and the world stopped spinning, Mark staggered to his feet. "Where's Amy?" He looked toward his truck. The door was open, and the cab was empty. "Amy!"

Matt caught him by the arm and probed at the aching goose egg at his temple. "I haven't seen her. Hold still."

"I sent her out to wait in my truck. There was a guy upstairs. I don't know what he hit me with." Oh, no. Hell no. He turned back to the porch.

"Amy must have ignored my warning and gone back in to help me. Amy!"

But Matt planted himself on the steps in front of him, blocking his path. "Uh-uh." He thumbed over his shoulder. "Fully engulfed. Neither of us is going back in there until the team comes with full gear."

Mark could see the flames shooting through an upstairs window and thick black smoke puffing out the front door. He turned 360 degrees, looking for a flag of copper-red hair. But there was nothing. He had her. The bastard who'd killed those women and taken pictures of Amy had her. "Lucky 13 isn't here yet?"

"They're en route. Two minutes out, according to Redding."

"Good. She hasn't been gone that long, then. He can't have gotten far."

"Gone?" Matt's tone was calm, but urgent. "Where? Where's Amy?"

Matt patted his pockets for his phone, then swore when he remembered he'd left it with Amy. "I can't call her."

Matt pulled out his cell. "Use mine."

Then Mark felt the lump in his front pocket. What the hell? He pulled out Amy's necklace, studied it in his hand. "She never takes this off."

A memory stirred in his foggy brain. *Rescue me, Fire Man.* He'd heard the words like he remembered a dream when he was about to wake up.

"I know where she is." He stuffed the necklace into his pocket.

"All right, let's go."

"No." He put up his hand to stop his brother. There was more than one threat here, and Mark couldn't stop them both. Amy had already lost enough. "I don't want to panic him, in case he hurts her." He ran around the side of the house, glimpsing the copper roof of Amy's art studio. "You got an ax in your truck?"

Matt was back in a matter of seconds and handed it to him. "You sure you don't want me to do this? I'm ninety-nine percent sure you've got a concussion."

"No. You take care of the fire." Mark swung the ax, gripping the handle in both hands before moving up the hill. "This is personal."

AMY SAT ON the edge of the sofa, chewing at the ropes Richie had tied around her wrists. He seemed inordinately interested in standing up to the copper garden alien she'd been sculpting. He thumped his chest against the sculpture's copper chest piece and laughed when it rattled. He picked up nearly every piece of glass and trash she'd sorted into various cubbies, sliding a couple into his pockets and tossing aside others.

Her first goal was freeing herself from the ropes that were cutting into her skin. The next step would be finding a way to unlock the padlocks he'd installed inside both the front and garage doors. Of course, she'd have to get past Richie himself first. And while she believed she could outthink him, he'd already proved that she couldn't outmuscle him.

And then she wanted to get back to the house. She wanted to get Mark out of there before the flames consumed him, before he suffocated, before she lost him forever. As tears stung her eyes and panic welled inside her, Amy angrily shoved them aside.

One problem at a time.

Now Richie had discovered her welding equipment. He clicked her lighter on several times, grinning each time it sparked a tiny flame. Fortunately, he set it aside before moving on to the tanks. He turned each valve on, hissing along with the release of the gas, inhaling a sinusful from each tank. "You shouldn't leave them on like that," she warned, keeping her voice as friendly as possible. Since the windows and doors were all locked shut, she could smell the gases gathering inside the building. "It isn't safe. It will eat up the oxygen and you could pass out. Or cause an explosion if you're not careful."

She dutifully dropped her hands to her lap when he turned to her. He still carried that mallet he'd used to hammer paint cans shut, swinging it through the air and pounding it down on different surfaces inside her studio, as though he enjoyed hearing the different sounds of smashing, bending and breaking.

"I like fire." Why wasn't that a surprise? "I don't know if I like explosions."

When he picked up a pry bar to pop off the brass tokens she'd used for eyes on her alien sculpture, Amy went back to work on the knot at her wrists.

"You found my treasures. You took them from me and gave them to Mr. O'Brien. I want some of your treasures to put in my box."

"I'll give you anything you want here, Richie. Just let me go."

He dropped his gaze to her hands in her lap, shaking his head as if he knew what she'd been doing all along. "You weren't nice to me. You gave away my treasures."

The strongbox with the incriminating evidence. She'd thought Dale O'Brien had murdered those women. He'd just been anxious to remove anything that would link him to the fires. Maybe he'd even suspected that Brad or Richie had killed Lissette, but if anyone found out he'd hired them, they might think he was the killer. "Those are your pictures? Your fire-starting kit?"

"The cotton balls are just to start the fire. But stain and turpentine burn really well once you get it lit." He sat down beside her, bumping his leg against hers. She didn't bother trying to slide away because he still held the mallet, and she'd seen the dent in Jocelyn's skull. "Mr. O'Brien paid Brad and me to burn down your stuff. Drive down the property value, or plain ol' scare you away from wantin' to stay. He said you and Miss Comfort had something he wanted." He plucked her braid from her shoulder and ran his fingers along its length. "You have something I want, too."

Amy breathed deeply through her nose, swallowing the urge to gag or run away as Richie caressed her hair.

"So, O'Brien is responsible for those fires." She intended to get that man arrested and as far away from her and her gran as she could. If she got away from Richie. Amy pushed the doubt out of her head. *When* she got away from Richie. Except for the ropes. And the locks. And the mallet. "You killed my friend Jocelyn. And Lissette."

"They were nice to me."

"You killed them because they were nice to you?"

"Like you're nice to me. Touching me. Smiling. Talking." His hand fisted around her braid, pulling painfully on her scalp. "Only you don't mean it any more than they did." He leaned in and rubbed a wet, juvenile kiss against her neck. "You're gonna be nice to me, aren't you, Miss Amy? The way you were nice to that fireman of yours?"

Amy watched his grip loosen on the mallet as he pulled her hair to turn her mouth to his.

No. No man was going to hurt her again.

Summoning her courage, letting her anger at too many injustices fuel her strength, Amy rammed her elbow into Richie's nose. As he cried out in pain and grabbed at his face, she rose, grabbing the mallet and slinging it as hard as she could across the room.

She ran to her workbench. She knew the weapon she needed to keep Richie away from her. She knew the tool she needed to cut her way through those locks. He'd already done half the work for her by turning on her oxyacetylene tanks. As long as the air hadn't truly filled with gas, she could do this without blowing herself up.

"Miss Amy!" With blood dripping from his broken nose, Richie lunged after her. If he hadn't wasted precious seconds looking for his weapon of choice and not finding the mallet, he would have reached her. "That wasn't nice!"

She dived for the lighter. Although she was hindered by her bound hands, she'd done this so often that she created a spark on the second strike. She grabbed the nearest hose.

Richie's hands were in her hair when she lit the torch and whirled around, bringing the cutting fire down over his arm and freeing herself. The torch hummed with power as she swung it again, aiming for one of those sunburned cheeks.

He staggered back, burned and bleeding, as she dragged the tank from its shelf. It crashed to the floor, disconnecting the hose. The torch went out and she dropped it, reaching for the lighter and igniting the second torch. It was impossible to aim the torch and carry the canister to the door with her hands tied.

Hold him off with the torch? Or run to the locked door?

Richie had the mallet in his fist again when he kicked aside a stool and screamed at her. "Why won't you be nice?"

Amy dropped the torch and ran to the door. "Help me! Somebody help!"

She rattled the padlock in useless frustration, wondering why Richie hadn't tackled her to the floor and smashed her head in already. Then she turned.

And realized the error she'd made.

Richie Sterling had dropped his mallet and picked up the burning flame of her welding torch. He ran the flame across her workbench, setting the wood on fire. Her drawings and desk went next.

"Richie, please!" She ran to the garage door and had no luck with the lock there, either.

He was going to burn this whole place down. He didn't care if he died. So long as the woman who'd been too mean to love him or make out with him or whatever misguided obsession he wanted to live out died, too.

He was at the sofa now, lighting it on fire and watching the flames.

The pry bar.

Amy blinked away the tears she had no time to shed and searched the floor to find the pry bar Richie had used and discarded. She'd slipped it behind the latch of the garage door when she heard a crash from the studio's front door.

She spun around as the wood splintered. Richie turned, too, holding the blinding torch in front of him like a flamethrower.

Something heavy smashed into the door again, breaking through. She saw the glint of a shiny ax head reflecting the flames from the fire. It disappeared and then crashed through the door again, sending it flying off its hinges.

And then Mark was there. Battered and bleeding, strong and every bit the heroic nickname she teased him with. "Amy!"

"Mark! Look out!"

Richie rushed toward him, but Mark was ready. Before the flame ever reached him, he jabbed the ax forward, hitting Richie square in the chest and knocking him back into the flames. He screamed and tried to escape, but the fire he loved was climbing the walls, surrounding him, consuming him.

Amy ran to Mark, pushing him toward the broken door. "Gas!"

He smelled it, too. He glanced down at her bound hands, and then, without so much as a grunt of effort, he swung her up into his arms and ran. The studio exploded behind them, knocking them both to the ground. His arms snapped around her to break their fall and they rolled several feet until they came to a stop with Amy lying on top of him.

Mark squeezed his eyes shut and tipped his head back into the dry grass, obviously working through some kind of pain.

"Mark?" Amy tried to frame his face between her hands, but the ropes wouldn't allow her to do more than cup his chin and run her fingers across his lips. "Mark? Are you okay? How badly are you hurt?"

His smoky blue eyes popped open and he lifted his head to kiss her. They were breathless from exertion and the kiss was short, but there was no doubting the clarity in his eyes or the laughter bubbling up from his throat. "Damn, woman. You *are* a lot of trouble."

And then they were sitting up and she was laughing, too. He untied her wrists and inspected the rope burns there. "Your pale skin shows every mark." He kissed the injuries, kissed her mouth, even as she tried to inspect the knot and dried blood at his temple.

"Do you get hurt every time you fight a fire?"

"I'm fine," he assured her. "I will be fine," he corrected. "Now that I know you're safe."

"How? How did you know where to find me?"

He dangled her pendant from his hand—his beautiful, perfect hand. "I got your message."

A trio of firefighters ran past them with a hose. When one of them stopped to ask how badly they were hurt, Mark waved them on to her studio. "Man inside. Probably didn't make it."

With a promise to check to see if Richie had survived, the man ran on. Mark reached for Amy's hand and pulled her to her feet. "Come on. We're in the way here. I want the medics to check you out."

"You, too." She'd make sure of that.

But the Lucky 13 fire engines parked in her driveway and in the yard in front of the house weren't the only flashing lights she saw. "Are those police cars at Dale O'Brien's place?"

"I bet they're taking O'Brien and Brad Frick in for questioning."

"O'Brien paid Brad and Richie to set fires on our property."

"I suspected as much."

"Richie saw the fires as an opportunity to hide his crimes when his…obsessive crushes…didn't work out." Mark pulled her to his side and got her walking toward the ambulance again, avoiding the firefighters who were fighting a losing battle to save her grandmother's historic home. "I don't think he understood how people work, how to interact in a normal, healthy way. I almost feel sorry for him."

"I don't. I almost lost you because of him."

"*I* almost lost *you*."

"Matt will make sure the paramedics clear me, or he'll drive me to the hospital himself."

"I like Matt."

"No. You like *me*."

"I do. So does my grandmother. That's a good sign, I think." She jerked when a timber cracked and fell inside the house. "Gran's going to miss that house."

Mark kept her tucked to his side as they watched the destruction. "I think she'd rather have you than the house."

Amy turned her face to Mark's shoulder. "So, are we ever going to go out on that date?"

"I'm the one who keeps asking." He pressed a kiss to her temple, then turned her away from the sad loss of her childhood home. "I think this is more than a heat-of-the-moment, opposites-attracting kind of thing."

Amy nodded. "I guess you had to rescue me after all." She laid her hand over the strong beat of his heart. "But I need you to love me even more."

Mark pulled her into his arms. "Done."

* * * * *

Look for the next book in
USA TODAY *bestselling author Julie Miller's*
duo, The Taylor Clan: Firehouse 13,
when Dead Man District
goes on sale next month.

And be sure to check out the stories featuring
the other Taylor brothers, Alex and Pike:

Man with the Muscle
Task Force Bride

Available now from Harlequin Intrigue!

Get 4 FREE REWARDS!

We'll send you 2 FREE Books plus 2 FREE Mystery Gifts.

Harlequin Romantic Suspense books are heart-racing page-turners with unexpected plot twists and irresistible chemistry that will keep you guessing to the very end.

FREE
Value Over
$20

YES! Please send me 2 FREE Harlequin Romantic Suspense novels and my 2 FREE gifts (gifts are worth about $10 retail). After receiving them, if I don't wish to receive any more books, I can return the shipping statement marked "cancel." If I don't cancel, I will receive 4 brand-new novels every month and be billed just $4.99 per book in the U.S. or $5.74 per book in Canada. That's a savings of at least 13% off the cover price! It's quite a bargain! Shipping and handling is just 50¢ per book in the U.S. and $1.25 per book in Canada.* I understand that accepting the 2 free books and gifts places me under no obligation to buy anything. I can always return a shipment and cancel at any time. The free books and gifts are mine to keep no matter what I decide.

240/340 HDN GNMZ

Name (please print)

Address   Apt. #

City   State/Province   Zip/Postal Code

Email: Please check this box ☐ if you would like to receive newsletters and promotional emails from Harlequin Enterprises ULC and its affiliates. You can unsubscribe anytime.

Mail to the **Reader Service:**
IN U.S.A.: P.O. Box 1341, Buffalo, NY 14240-8531
IN CANADA: P.O. Box 603, Fort Erie, Ontario L2A 5X3

Want to try 2 free books from another series? Call 1-800-873-8635 or visit www.ReaderService.com.

---

*Terms and prices subject to change without notice. Prices do not include sales taxes, which will be charged (if applicable) based on your state or country of residence. Canadian residents will be charged applicable taxes. Offer not valid in Quebec. This offer is limited to one order per household. Books received may not be as shown. Not valid for current subscribers to Harlequin Romantic Suspense books. All orders subject to approval. Credit or debit balances in a customer's account(s) may be offset by any other outstanding balance owed by or to the customer. Please allow 4 to 6 weeks for delivery. Offer available while quantities last.

Your Privacy—Your information is being collected by Harlequin Enterprises ULC, operating as Reader Service. For a complete summary of the information we collect, how we use this information and to whom it is disclosed, please visit our privacy notice located at corporate.harlequin.com/privacy-notice. From time to time we may also exchange your personal information with reputable third parties. If you wish to opt out of this sharing of your personal information, please visit readerservice.com/consumerschoice or call 1-800-873-8635. **Notice to California Residents**—Under California law, you have specific rights to control and access your data. For more information on these rights and how to exercise them, visit corporate.harlequin.com/california-privacy.

HRS20R2

Get 4 FREE REWARDS!

We'll send you 2 FREE Books plus 2 FREE Mystery Gifts.

Harlequin Presents books feature the glamorous lives of royals and billionaires in a world of exotic locations, where passion knows no bounds.

FREE Value Over $20

Get 4 FREE REWARDS!

We'll send you 2 FREE Books <u>plus</u> 2 FREE Mystery Gifts.

FREE
Value Over
$20

Both the **Romance** and **Suspense** collections feature compelling novels written by many of today's bestselling authors.

YES! Please send me 2 FREE novels from the Essential Romance or Essential Suspense Collection and my 2 FREE gifts (gifts are worth about $10 retail). After receiving them, if I don't wish to receive any more books, I can return the shipping statement marked "cancel." If I don't cancel, I will receive 4 brand-new novels every month and be billed just $7.24 each in the U.S. or $7.49 each in Canada. That's a savings of up to 28% off the cover price. It's quite a bargain! Shipping and handling is just 50¢ per book in the U.S. and $1.25 per book in Canada.* I understand that accepting the 2 free books and gifts places me under no obligation to buy anything. I can always return a shipment and cancel at any time. The free books and gifts are mine to keep no matter what I decide.

Choose one: ☐ **Essential Romance**   ☐ **Essential Suspense**
                      (194/394 MDN GQ6M)   (191/391 MDN GQ6M)

Name (please print)

Address   Apt. #

City   State/Province   Zip/Postal Code

Email: Please check this box ☐ if you would like to receive newsletters and promotional emails from Harlequin Enterprises ULC and its affiliates. You can unsubscribe anytime.

Mail to the **Reader Service:**
IN U.S.A.: P.O. Box 1341, Buffalo, NY 14240-8531
IN CANADA: P.O. Box 603, Fort Erie, Ontario L2A 5X3

Want to try 2 free books from another series! Call 1-800-873-8635 or visit www.ReaderService.com.

*Terms and prices subject to change without notice. Prices do not include sales taxes, which will be charged (if applicable) based on your state or country of residence. Canadian residents will be charged applicable taxes. Offer not valid in Quebec. This offer is limited to one order per household. Books received may not be as shown. Not valid for current subscribers to the Essential Romance or Essential Suspense Collection. All orders subject to approval. Credit or debit balances in a customer's account(s) may be offset by any other outstanding balance owed by or to the customer. Please allow 4 to 6 weeks for delivery. Offer available while quantities last.

Your Privacy—Your information is being collected by Harlequin Enterprises ULC, operating as Reader Service. For a complete summary of the information we collect, how we use this information and to whom it is disclosed, please visit our privacy notice located at corporate.harlequin.com/privacy-notice. From time to time we may also exchange your personal information with reputable third parties. If you wish to opt out of this sharing of your personal information, please visit readerservice.com/consumerschoice or call 1-800-873-8635. **Notice to California Residents**—Under California law, you have specific rights to control and access your data. For more information on these rights and how to exercise them, visit corporate.harlequin.com/california-privacy.

STRS20R2

Get 4 FREE REWARDS!

We'll send you 2 FREE Books <u>plus</u> 2 FREE Mystery Gifts.

Worldwide Library books feature gripping mysteries from "whodunits" to police procedurals and courtroom dramas.

FREE Value Over $20

THE 2020 CHRISTMAS ROMANCE COLLECTION!

'Tis the season for romance!

You're sure to fall in love with these tenderhearted love stories from some of your favorite bestselling authors!

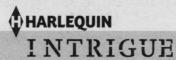
#1971 IMPACT ZONE
Tactical Crime Division: Traverse City • by Julie Anne Lindsey
TCD special agent Max McRay is the definition of *unflappable*. But when a serial bomber wreaks havoc in the town where his ex-wife, Allie, and infant son live, suddenly a high-profile case becomes personal.

#1972 HOMICIDE AT WHISKEY GULCH
The Outriders Series • by Elle James
When Delta Force soldier Trace Travis returns home after his father's murder, he partners with Lily Davidson, his high school sweetheart, to find his father's killer—and overcome the circumstances that have always kept them apart.

#1973 AGENT UNDER SIEGE
The Justice Seekers • by Lena Diaz
The police believe they have found Teagan Ray's kidnapper, but Teagan knows they're wrong. Former profiler Bryson Anton agrees to investigate, but soon their search results in brutal attacks from a cunning suspect...and a powerful mutual attraction.

#1974 THE FUGITIVE
A Marshal Law Novel • by Nichole Severn
When Raleigh Wilde reappears in Deputy Beckett Foster's life asking for his help to clear her name, he's shocked—even more so when he learns she's pregnant with his child. But a killer is willing to do anything to keep Raleigh from discovering who embezzled millions from the charity she runs...

#1975 DEAD MAN DISTRICT
The Taylor Clan: Firehouse 13 • by Julie Miller
Firefighter Matt Taylor's new neighbor, Corie McGuire, makes Matt want to focus on the present. Her troubled son, Evan, reminds Matt of his younger self. When the boy is implicated in a string of fires, Matt vows to help. Is Evan guilty...or has Corie's past come back to threaten them all?

#1976 ALASKA MOUNTAIN RESCUE
A K-9 Alaska Novel • by Elizabeth Heiter
Alanna Morgan was raised by kidnappers in remote Alaska. But now she's hunting for her criminal "mother" with Peter Robak, a cop who trusts her as little as she trusts him. As they investigate, she and Peter begin to move past old traumas to deeply connect...while danger looms at every turn.

HICNM1220